Ned: Barnardo Boy

by

Barbara Coyle

2

Dedication

To Aidan, Eoin, Molly, and Deirdre
Who, like Ned, have come from overseas
to be our children

Author's Note

In the first chapter of *Anne of Green Gables*, Marilla says, "At first Matthew suggested getting a Barnardo boy. But I said 'no' flat to that. 'They may be all right—I'm not saying they're not—but no London street Arabs for me,' I said."

That paragraph was my first introduction to the term "Barnardo boy," and it was not until many years afterward that I discovered what it meant and what "London street Arabs" had to do with getting farm help in Canada. I hope you enjoy the discovery as much as I did. Many, many thanks are due to several people:

Sarah Jones, for her invaluable help with the London section of the book (even visiting the Ragged School Museum on my behalf!)

David Ghent and George Janzen (my dad), for their inestimable help with the Canadian section of the book

Jeena Lim, for her advice, encouragement and feedback every step of the way, and whose flattering enthusiasm was probably my greatest single motivator.

And thanks are due to all those who pre-read and proofread this book, giving great feedback and finding the errors my eyes missed.

Barbara Coyle
Co. Longford, Ireland

Chapter 1

Shoreditch, London, 1876

"'E re you are, gov'ner," said the cabbie as he let the young man out of his cab and took his fare. "Mead Street. Watch yoursel' now." He clucked to his horse and the cab moved on.

The young man had known before he came that he would need to "watch himself," and he took a firm grip on his walking stick. His position as a clerk to a solicitor[1] often required that he find certain people, but never had he been in a neighbourhood as poor as this. He looked at his map again. Yes, Foundry Lane was just off Mead Street. He picked his way past the piles of rubbish that lay around the doorways—old boots, empty wine bottles, and rags—and tried not to stumble over the small children who were playing in the filthy gutter. The air in London was never what one could call pure, but the smells here were absolutely putrid.

---

[1] Solicitor= lawyer

It was a sunny day for January, and though the air was cold many of the dwellings had their doors open. This was to try to get rid of the "bad air" which everyone believed caused so much of the sickness in that district. He peeped into one or two of the open doors and saw rooms with nearly nothing in them. He walked the length of Mead Street twice without seeing a single sign to show him which of the alleys that led off the main street might be Foundry Lane. He asked a few of the men who were lounging about in doorways if they knew the location of Foundry Lane, but they shook their heads.

But it must *be along here somewhere*, he said to himself, and as he wondered who might be able to enlighten him, he saw a policeman.

"Certainly, sir," said the policeman when the question had been put to him. "But you won't find it by asking for Foundry Lane—it's known as Button-hole Row to those that live there."

"Ah. Well, do you know how to find Button-hole Row, then?"

"Yes, sir. Do you recall seeing a pub called the Dog and Duck? Well, just beyond it is a little doorway that looks like it leads to nothing, but if you go in there you'll soon find yourself in Button-hole Row."

"Thank you," said the young man.

"You will take care, sir, won't you?" added the policeman. "It's not the most law-abiding place in the district."

"I will, indeed."

The young man found the little doorway and discovered that it led into a kind of courtyard where ten or more brick houses were crammed together around a tiny central square. He took a paper from his pocket and looked at the name written there: Mrs. Amelia Miller. *I suppose I must just ask if anyone knows her*, he thought.

A woman was sitting in the doorway of the house nearest to him, sewing on a small piece of cloth. Beside her, on another stool, was a girl of about nine who was sewing on a similar piece of cloth. Both glanced up at the stranger as he approached them, but then looked down at their work and kept their eyes on their sewing.

"Pardon me," the young man began, "Do you know of a Mrs. Amelia Miller who lives in Foundry Lane—or, I suppose, Button-hole Row?"

"I do," said the woman, "Or I did. She's dead these two weeks."

"Dead!"

"Died o' consumption last Tuesday week, God rest 'er."

"You're certain?"

A smile flickered over the woman's face, though she still kept her eyes on her work.

"Sure as anything. I saw 'er buried."

"Well," said the young man, "I suppose my task is finished, then. I'll tell the solicitor that she's not in need of money anymore."

"Money?" said the woman, looking up for a moment before dropping her eyes to her needle again.

"She was a servant at one time, I believe," said the young man. "Her former employer left her a small sum in his will, and it was my duty to find her and give her what was due her. Not now," he added hastily, as he suddenly remembered that thieves were thick in these parts and might rob him for the money they thought he carried, "but after her identity could be proven."

The woman sighed. "She could ha' done with a bit o' money, poor soul. Many's the time we've sat together sewing all night to get the rent money before it come due. She 'ad no children to keep, but then, no children to help 'er, either. Katie here earns two or three shillin' a week."

The man looked at the girl and saw a smaller version of her mother. She also had the round shoulders that came with constant stooping, the dress well flecked with ends of cotton thread, and the swiftly moving fingers.

"Does it take long to earn three shillings, then?" asked the man.

The woman shrugged. "Three halfpence for button-holing a dozen collars is small pay. You see," she went on, taking a fresh collar from her pocket to show him, "the holes is just raw cuts, an' we have to stitch all round them an' make the button-holes. A single button-hole don't look much, but there are three holes in every collar; that's thirty-six in the dozen—six holes to work for a farthing². An' we buy our own thread as well." She finished the collar she was working on, laid it aside, and took another one out of her large apron pocket.

While she was speaking the young man had been mentally calculating the quantity of work required to earn the sum she had named. "Why, you must have to do *one thousand four hundred and forty button-holes* to earn even five shillings! How can you have time to eat or sleep?"

The woman shrugged again. "I work fifteen hours a day, and Katie four or five. She's a minder for a baby when she's not button-holing. We can earn ten shillings a week, which is more than most hereabouts."

The man was about to exclaim again, but was prevented by the woman's saying fondly, "There you are, Neddy!"

---

² farthing: ¼ penny. It was originally called a "fourthling" and eventually became "farthing."

Looking about him, the young man saw a little boy, about three or four years old, coming across the courtyard. The little boy was filthy and dressed in rags, but there was a sweet expression on his face.

"Are you hungry, luv?" said the woman, and when the boy nodded, she said, "Take 'im into the house, Katie, and give 'im a bun."

"Is he yours as well?" asked the young man.

"No, no, I've only got Katie. Neddy's nobody's child."

"Nobody's child?"

"That's right. No parents or family."

"But where does he live?"

"Oh, he sleeps here and there—most o' the women in the Row have a bit o' kindness about them, and they lets him sleep on their floors and gives him a bite of food when he comes around."

"But where did he come from?"

The woman shook her head. "I dunno. There's lots of nobody's children, and who's to say how any of 'em got here?"

"And what will happen to him?"

The woman shook her head again.

The young man was silent for a moment, watching the woman's fingers swiftly pushing the needle in and out of the cloth. Katie had returned to her stool and was sewing just as rapidly as her mother. And the little boy Neddy was sitting on the floor between them, devouring his little brown bun. Slowly the man reached into his pocket and pulled out a shilling.

"Here," he said, holding it out. "That's to buy him some food." And before the woman could thank him, he walked quickly away.

Chapter 2

The morning dawned clear on the day that the newspapers were dated July 25, 1879. The headlines proclaimed the news of a decisive British victory in the Zulu war. The Zulus were utterly defeated, having lost at least a thousand warriors while only ten British soldiers had been killed.

On that morning it was the sound of the costers[3] going to work that woke Ned. Cautiously he crawled out from beneath the overturned barrow where he had found shelter the night before, looking this way and that to see that no policeman was in sight. It was against the law to be a vagrant, and more than one boy of his acquaintance had been brought before the court to be charged as such. Satisfied that he had escaped detection yet again, he stretched luxuriously in the early morning sunlight. It wasn't so bad to sleep in the streets in the summer. It wasn't bitterly cold, and the sun could light his way as he went to his work.

---

[3] Coster = short for "costermonger": seller of vegetables, fruits and fish. Many had barrows and went through the streets, others had permanent stalls.

For Ned was a working boy. The intervening years had taken away the sweet expression from his face and replaced it with a worldly-wise one. He had grown—a little—and his place as the darling of Button-hole Row had been taken by younger urchins than he. But all things considered, he was not a bad boy. The women in Button-hole Row had been proud of the fact that they worked for their money instead of begging or stealing it, though some of them did those things as well. Ned had caught this attitude, and tried to earn an honest farthing to feed himself. If he couldn't earn it, well... he *had* sometimes stolen something. But, he reasoned, not near as often as other boys.

Ned's chosen occupation was that of parcel-carrier, and his usual place of business was the train station. Sometimes he lingered on the streets near the shops, but there were more boys trying to carry parcels there. The train station was further away and Ned tried to get there to meet the first train of the day. If he earned enough, he would be able to buy some food in a few hours.

He was in time today: the first passengers were just coming out of the station door. The first gentleman out carried nothing but a walking stick, but the second man had a box.

"Carry yer box, sir?" said Ned, tugging at his cap respectfully.

The middle-aged man paused mid-step and looked at Ned.

"Well, I suppose so, for a little way. It is a heavy box. Can you manage it?"

"Oh, yes, sir!" said Ned eagerly, and reached out for the box.

It *was* rather heavy, but Ned trotted along next to the gentleman without complaining. If he could carry it a long way for him, he might earn as much as a penny. That would be enough to buy a small meat pie, a very great treat indeed! After ten minutes' walk, Ned was out of his usual neighbourhood. He kept a close eye on the streets they were taking, so that he would know how to get back again. The box seemed to be getting heavier as he went on. It was too large for him to tuck under an arm; he had to carry it with both hands in front of his chest.

After fifteen minutes Ned's arms were trembling and he began to be afraid that he would drop the box. His legs were tired, too. He hoped the gentleman was nearly to his destination.

The man looked at Ned. "You're getting tired, child. I'll carry it from here."

"Oh, no, sir, I ain't tired! I can carry it all the way for you!" He tried to lift the box higher and move his feet faster to prove his point.

"You're a plucky boy, I will say that. A box with several books in it is quite a load. What's your name?"

"Ned."

"And how old are you?"

"I dunno."

The man nodded. *He looks about five,* he thought to himself, *but he's more likely six or seven. He has that pinched face and scrawny body—classic malnutrition, as Dr. Phillips would say.*

"Did you ever go to school?"

"No, sir. I got to work."

Yes, thought the gentleman, *you look as if you couldn't scrape together the few pence a week it would take to go to school.*

"Where is it that you live?"

Ned gave him a quick, speculative glance. The man appeared kindly, but would he turn him in to the police?

The man understood the look. "I mean, where is your neighbourhood? Bishopsgate?"

"Shoreditch, sir."

"There's no Ragged School in Shoreditch?"

"Not as I knows on."

Ned stumbled. Chagrined, he gripped the box tighter and walked as fast as he could, trying to keep his panting quiet. What if the gentleman took it away from him now?

"We're nearly there, Ned," said the man, letting him continue.

After another hundred feet, the man halted in front of a house. "Here's where I stop," said the man. Ned gave up the box, allowing his aching arms to fall by his side.

"Here's your pay, and it was a job well done," said the man, dropping two pennies into Ned's hand. "You ought to go to school, if you can," he continued. "You'd make good if you kept at it the way you've carried that box. Good day to you." And the man went inside the house.

Ned looked at the two bronze coins in his hand. He could buy *two* pies! It had been months since he'd had that much food at once. He would get them from Mr. Abel, who kept the best pie-shop in Shoreditch. In spite of his weariness, he made the journey back quickly. He had been hungry all morning—indeed, he had been hungry for most of yesterday, too. The gnawing hunger pangs in his stomach seemed to grow worse with the anticipation of food. He passed a pie-shop and hesitated. Should he eat here? He nearly succumbed to the temptation, but the thought of Mr. Abel's pies decided him. He would wait.

He was nearly there when he saw Thunder John. His heart sank. Of all the big boys on the street, Thunder John was the most dangerous. He was an accomplished thief and the best fighter in Shoreditch. Nothing was safe from him. Ned grasped his pennies tighter and glanced quickly around. Perhaps he could hide! But where? There was no barrow or wagon or crate nearby, and not even a crevice between the tightly-packed buildings. There was a lamppost; it would have to do. Hastily he dodged behind it and tried to make his body as skinny and straight as he could. If Thunder John was not really looking in his direction, he might not be seen.

His forehead touching the lamppost, he held his breath and waited for what seemed like an hour. Just when he had decided that Thunder John must have passed by without seeing him, he felt a tap on his shoulder.

"Boy." The deep voice could belong to no one else. Ned turned and looked up into Thunder John's face. "What are you doin' there?"

"Nuthin'."

Thunder John laughed and glanced at Ned's clenched fist. "And what's in your hand?"

"Nuthin'."

"Give it to me."

There was nothing to do but to hand over the two precious coins. The slightest protest from Ned would have earned him a blow on the face from Thunder John's lightning fist. Without a word, the bully turned away and continued down the street.

Ned lowered himself to the ground, still leaning against the lamppost. He would have cried if he had not been so tired. As it was, a tear escaped from his eye and trickled down his face. He wiped it away quickly. *I'll get up in a moment,* he told himself; *just as soon as I've rested a little bit. I might get another parcel to carry...*

"Ned!"

He looked up and saw Jack.

"You had any grub?"

Ned only shook his head.

"Me neither." Jack leaned against the lamppost, still holding his broom. He was a crossing-sweeper.

"How's trade this morning?" asked Ned.

"Bad. It's not mucky enough for the gents and ladies to want to pay for a sweep."

Ned nodded. While there was no doubt that wet weather was more uncomfortable for homeless boys, it was better for the business of crossing-sweepers. When the mud and filth on the roads made the shoes of quality people impossibly dirty they were more willing to pay a boy who tried to clear a path across the road for them.

"I saw the greengrocer sweeping out just now," said Jack. "There's like to be a turnip or carrot somewheres in there."

Ned got up. "Better try it," he said. The boys walked a block to the corner of Bethnal Green Road, where Jack was crossing sweeper. The pile of refuse that the greengrocer had swept out was still in the gutter, and the boys picked through it. They were rewarded. Jack found an apple that was only half rotten, and Ned found a wilted carrot. They ate them while they continued to search for other morsels. All they found were a few more vegetables too slimy and rotten to tempt even their hungry stomachs.

Jack took up his broom again and went back to work, dodging the carriages, vans, and horses while he cleared a path through the muck that had accumulated on the road in the last hour. Ned went back to the station and tried to find another parcel to carry. It took three hours, but at last a lady did pay him a half-pence to carry her bag for a short distance. It was enough to buy a small fried fish and a cup of coffee from a coffee stall.

As he stood in the street drinking the hot coffee, a coster with eel pies came down the road, calling, "Here's all hot! Toss or buy! Up and win 'em!" One of the big boys, whom Ned knew as Alf, sauntered up to the pieman. "I'll toss," he said and pulled out a penny. The pieman said, "Heads!" as Alf tossed the coin in the air. Those standing around looked at the coin as it fell to the ground.

"Tails!" called out one, and there was general laughter at Alf's misfortune. Alf shrugged his shoulders and meandered off, while the pieman pocketed the penny and moved on, calling out, "Hot eel pies! Toss or buy!"

Ned had tried tossing with a pieman—once. If you won the toss, you got the pie for free, but if you lost, you got nothing and lost your penny. It wasn't worth the risk to Ned. The older boys were more likely to bet, but they lost as often as not. He had heard a pieman say that sometimes drunken gentlemen would toss for a pie and if they won they would throw the pies at each other or at him.

His coffee finished, Ned went back to the station to see if he could earn enough to buy a bun, but two hours of respectful requests for work brought no rewards. He wondered if Jack had had any luck and wandered toward Bethnal Green Road. The traffic—both people and vehicle—was increasing as places of business closed for the day and people made their way home. He found Jack on his corner, waiting for a lull in the stream of omnibuses and cabs.

"I got a bit," said Jack. "A few farthings for sweeping, and then a gentleman sent me with a message and gave me a brown[4]." It was one of the benefits of always sweeping the same corner—the people who usually crossed the street there and recognized him would sometimes send him on errands. Just then he spotted an opening and he darted into the street, sweeping furiously a few paces in front of a well-dressed man. He tugged at his forelock politely as they reached the

---

[4] Brown = half-penny

other side of the road, but the man passed him without a glance. As Ned stood watching, he saw a woman crossing the street toward him with her arms full of parcels. She nearly dropped one of them as she stepped onto the kerb.

"Carry yer parcels, ma'am?" said Ned.

"Well," she hesitated, "Perhaps." Just then one of her parcels slid off its perch and Ned caught it as it fell.

"I suppose you'd better take a couple of them." She gave him two paper packages that were tied with string and set off briskly down the street. She didn't have very far to go, but Ned still received a half-pence for his service. He ran towards the baker's shop. There was a queue when he got there, and he waited his turn as patiently as he could.

As he neared the front of the queue, he could hear a girl crying and the baker saying, "Sorry, miss, I can't give you any more credit. You pay a bit of what you owe, and then we'll see. I know it ain't your fault, but I got my business to consider, see?"

The girl, who was carrying a toddler, left the shop still crying. Ned recognized her as Katie, whom he had known on Button-hole Row. He followed her outside, but before he could speak to her, another girl, holding a basket of oranges to sell, approached her to ask what the matter was.

"Oh, Mary! Mum sent me to see if we could get a bit o' bread from the baker on credit, but he won't have it."

"She's still bad, is she?"

"Worse, I think. She can hardly finish a dozen collars an hour."

Mary sucked in her breath. "That's bad, that is."

"And Mrs. Brody hasn't paid me for two weeks for mindin' Emmy. She's on the drink again."

"And she'll never come off it," said Mary sagely. "You'd better leave Emmy in the gin palace with her and find another baby to mind."

"I couldn't," said Katie. "Emmy wouldn't last a week if I gave 'er up."

"*You* won't last long if you've got nothin' to eat. What's your rent?"

"Four shillings. It's a foul room—I know the damp makes Mum worse, but there's nowheres else to go."

Ned tugged at Katie's dress until she turned to look at him, "There you are, Neddy," she said kindly, in spite of her tears.

"Here's a brown," he said, holding it out to her. "I had lots o' food today. I ain't hungry."

Katie bent and kissed the top of his head—dirty and matted as it was, which made Ned disappear down the street.

For the rest of the evening he "went for a turn around," which meant that he walked about in search of amusement. He saw two dogs fighting in an alley. He saw a drunken man staggering down the street. He saw a matchbox maker taking her stock of newly-made boxes to the factory to be filled with matches. And then he saw Tom, who was selling bootlaces, pick the pocket of a well-dressed young lady. Tom first asked her in the most beseeching tones to "buy a few laces off a poor orphan who hasn't a bit of bread to eat." She told him to go away, but he kept beside her, begging her assistance and making remarks about the ingratitude of the world in general and of young ladies in particular. Ned, who knew where it was all leading, tagged along behind to see the fun.

As Tom's manner became troublesome the lady threatened to give him over to the charge of a policeman, and looked down every area to find one. But there wasn't one, and the boy kept up his laments and now and then gave her a slight push with the basket on which he carried his laces. Then her hand went into her pocket; the purse was gone. She ran after the thief, who, knowing young ladies in fancy shoes were not made for running, ran away whistling. The young lady ran also, shouting "Stop, thief! Stop, thief!" But then fine young ladies are not particularly made for shouting, either, and there was no policeman nearby. The culprit got safely off with the purse and its contents.

As it was July, the sunlight did not completely disappear until St. George's chimes had struck ten o'clock. By then the gas street lights were all burning and Ned looked around to find a place to sleep. He found an overturned barrow, but looking under it he saw Jack, sleeping with his broom clutched in his hand. There was a shadowed doorway nearby, and Ned sat down in it to rest for a while. He had dozed off for an hour or so when he heard a policeman's voice: "Move along, boy—no sleeping here!" Ned opened his eyes to see the policeman talking to the overturned barrow. He rapped on it with his truncheon. "Out with you! Move on!" And Jack crawled out from beneath the barrow with his broom and moved along to find another place to sleep. Ned waited for the policeman to discover and move him along, but the policeman didn't see him, and Ned drifted off again.

Chapter 3

Mr. Warren, the middle-aged man whose box Ned had carried, was thoughtful as he made his way home that day. As the minister of the Baptist church in Lower Holloway, he was used to seeing poverty of varying degrees, but he could not quite forget the dogged way the child had stuck to his work. He hoped the boy had got a good meal with the two pence he had earned.

As he neared his home his footsteps quickened, for home was very dear to him. His wife would be the first to greet him when he arrived, and his daughters would be next; Mary, Helen, Lydia, and Frances would be eager to tell him of the day's events. Betty, the maid-of-all-work, would not greet him, but she would smile when she came in to announce that supper was ready.

Though Ned would have thought Mr. Warren very rich indeed, he was not really very wealthy at all. His home was small and in an unfashionable part of London. The food his family ate was plain and inexpensive, and the clothes they wore were rarely new. They had no piano in their parlour, nor could they afford to keep their home very warm in the winter. But Mr. and Mrs. Warren found no hardship in all of this. They had once been much poorer and were thankful for the comforts they now had.

Mr. Warren was greeted by his family just as he had anticipated, and as he took his usual seat in the parlour, he looked around him with satisfaction at the neat room in which his family was gathering to speak to him. The walls were covered with a dark red wallpaper, and the doors and other woodwork were stained a dark brown. The carpet had a pattern of gold flowers with a brown background, and the heavy green curtains did an admirable job of keeping out the sunlight that would fade the sofa and armchairs. The brass fender and coal scuttle were clean, as it was summertime and no fire needed to be lit in the parlour.

"What do you think, Father?" began Frances, who at seven years old was the youngest. "A bad boy stole Lydia's bread and butter this morning on her way to school!"

"Stole Lydia's bread and butter?" repeated Mr. Warren.

"Yes, Father," said Lydia, who was ten.

"She was eating her bread and butter for elevenses[5] on the way to school," said Frances, rather too eagerly.

"Was she, indeed?" said Mr. Warren with a slight smile. "But I suspect the consequence was a just punishment for the offence. How did it happen, Lydia?"

"A ragged boy came and pushed me down and took my bread and butter and ran away!"

"He was probably very hungry," said Mr. Warren, thinking of Ned.

"But he ought not to steal, even if he is hungry," said Frances.

---

[5] elevenses: a snack time at about 11:00 am

"No, he ought not to. But perhaps he has no mother and father to tell him what is right and wrong."

"He ought to go to school, then, and his teacher could tell him not to steal!" said Lydia.

"Was the boy wearing shoes?"

Lydia bit her lip thoughtfully as she tried to remember. "No," she said, "I don't think he was."

"Then he wouldn't be allowed into school, would he?" said Mr. Warren. "Does *your* teacher let children with no shoes and ragged clothes come to school?"

"No, Father."

"But, Father," said Mary, who was fifteen, "Is that not very unfair to the poorest children to keep them from school? How could the poorest children possibly buy shoes?"

Mrs. Warren answered, "There is some good in those rules, Mary. Most children have families who can buy shoes, and who can send their children to school dressed in a neat and tidy way. It is good for the children to learn the importance of being clean and orderly. It is only the very poorest children who cannot go to a Board School. But even they can attend a Ragged School."

"What is a Ragged School?" asked Frances.

"It is a free school that is taught by charitable people. Children can come in whatever clothes they have, which is why they are called Ragged Schools."

"Then why do not the poor children all go to those schools?"

"Some of them must work," said Mr. Warren. "I met a little boy today who carried my box of books for me. He carried it from Shoreditch Station to Nicholas Street, and he looked to be only about six or seven. He didn't know how old he was, and I would imagine that he is an orphan. If he does not work, he will have nothing to eat."

"Did you give him some food?" asked Helen, who was thirteen and very tender-hearted.

"I gave him two pence and I hope he got a good meal out of it. I told him he ought to go to school, but he said he didn't know if there was a Ragged School in Shoreditch."

"I don't think there is anymore," said Mrs. Warren. "There used to be one in Brick Lane, but they gave it up when the Board School opened."

"Hmm," said Mr. Warren. "No doubt there's not as great a need for Ragged Schools as there used to be, but the poorest children still need education. I wonder if there is one in Bishopsgate or Bethnal Green."

"I know there is a small one in Bethnal Green—Derbyshire Street."

Just then Betty, the maid-of-all-work, came in to announce that supper was ready. The family gathered around the table, and after saying grace they filled their plates with German potatoes stuffed with sausages, boiled cabbage, and turnips.

"Do you suppose there are *many* hungry children in London tonight?" asked Helen as she looked at the food on her plate.

"I'm afraid there are," said her mother.

"I wish I could give some of them my food," said Helen.

Her father smiled in sympathy. "I often wish the same," he said. "I long to give a half-penny to every crossing sweeper or parcel carrier that I pass. But if I did so, I would part with a pound every time I go out!"

Mrs. Warren agreed. "We could easily give *all* our money away to those who are in want, but then who would feed our family?"

"Father, may I give my pennies to feed some poor children?" Frances wanted to know.

"Of course you may. Perhaps we could enquire if the Ragged School in Bethnal Green provides food for the pupils. If they do not, we might be able to help organize something of the kind. It might entice those children who must work for their bread to come to school."

Mrs. Warren smiled and said, "Perhaps we could start a little 'soup fund' along the lines of Mrs. Spurgeon's book fund."

The girls nodded their heads. The Reverend Charles Spurgeon's wife had begun a fund to pay for books for poor ministers who needed them. Mr. Warren himself had received books from Mrs. Spurgeon in the past.

"Mrs. Spurgeon began the book fund by saving every five shilling coin that came into her possession," continued Mrs. Warren. "I cannot save that much, but I could put by every thruppence that I receive."

"And I could put by every ha'penny!" said Helen, and so the "soup fund" for the benefit of poor children who had no food was begun.

When the food on the table was all eaten up, Betty handed round the dessert.

"Lydia made the apple dumplings," Mrs. Warren told her husband.

"Done to perfection," said Mr. Warren with a smile at his daughter. And they all savoured the baked apples in their little pastry crusts.

After dinner the kitchen was tidied and the family gathered in the parlour. Lydia recited "The Cock is Crowing," which she had learned at school, and then they listened to Mr. Warren read *Uncle Tom's Cabin* aloud. After family prayers, the girls went up to bed, thankful that although their food was plain, their clothes were not new, and their beds were shared, they at least had food, clothes, and beds...and parents who loved them.

Chapter 4

Mr. Warren made enquiries and discovered that the Ragged School in Derbyshire Street, Bethnal Green, had no money for providing food for its scholars. The school had been founded and supported by members of a Methodist church in Bethnal Green, but funds were very low. Since the government had, a few years before, organised school boards and founded many schools—called board schools—in the effort to bring education to all children, many Ragged Schools had closed, and interest in supporting those schools had waned.

It took Mr. Warren three months to stir up enough interest in the project to raise the money needed to provide food for the pupils: a slice of bread and butter when they arrived and soup at the dinner hour.

Mr. Warren did not often go to Shoreditch, but he was in that neighbourhood a week before the school was to start providing food. He had not seen Ned since that day in July, but today when he arrived at the train station he made a point of looking for the boy. He did not see him at first and was about to leave when he found him sitting on the ground by the corner of the station with his eyes closed.

Ned was tired. It was nearly noon and he had not yet had any work or anything to eat. And it was cold.

"Hello there, Ned," said Mr. Warren. "Are you looking for work?"

Ned's eyes opened and he got to his feet. "Yessir," he said quickly. He did not recognize Mr. Warren as one of his usual customers and rather wondered at his knowing what his name was.

"Tell me, then," said Mr. Warren, "Do you know of a bakery—a good one—around Derbyshire Street?"

"Yessir. Hobbes' bakery is as good as any."

"Can you lead me to it?"

"Of course, sir!"

Ned led the way. Mr. Warren glanced at the boy as they walked along. He did not look as well as he had last summer. He was walking more slowly, even as he tried to give the impression of briskness, and his eyes seemed to be sunken into his face.

"Do you go to school?"

The question stirred Ned's memory. Had not someone asked him that question before? He gave the same answer: "No, sir, I got to work."

"But what will you do for work when you are older, Ned, if you have no learning?"

Ned looked again at the man. Was this the one who had paid him so well for carrying a box in the summer? "Oh, I dunno," he answered, rather cheerfully than otherwise. Then, after a pause, he added, "A coster, or somethin' o' that kind, if I'm lucky."

"And if you are not lucky?"

"If I ain't lucky," he repeated hesitatingly. "Well, if I ain't lucky, I must take my chance; I'll have to live somehow, same as others."

"There's a Ragged School in Bethnal Green, in Derbyshire Street," said Mr. Warren. "It isn't so far from where you live. Would you go there?"

Ned shrugged his shoulders. He had seen children on their way to school, carrying slates and books and dressed in stiff and uncomfortable clothes. Those children were no doubt warmer than he was, but he had no desire to give up his freedom in order to sit in a schoolroom. And then how would he get any food?

"I got to work," he said again.

"The school will provide dinners," said Mr. Warren, and Ned's head jerked up to look at him.

"For anyone?"

"Anyone who comes to the school."

"And anyone can come to the school?"

"Anyone."

Ned smiled for the first time at Mr. Warren. "I'll come, sir, an' I'll bring Katie an' Emmy an' Jack."

They walked along Church Street until they reached Abbey Street. Hobbes' bakery, as usual, had a queue of people waiting, and Mr. Warren kept Ned with him while he waited his turn. He noticed Ned's eyes following every article of food that customers carried out of the bakery.

"Two muffins[6], please," said Mr. Warren, when it was his turn. "And may I speak to the proprietor about placing a daily order for bread?" He was given the muffins, and he offered them both to Ned, who ate them rapidly while Mr. Warren spoke to the owner. When the

---

[6] muffins = the kind that Americans would call English muffins

business was completed, Mr. Warren said, "Come and see where the school is." So they walked back up Abbey Street and along Derbyshire Street until they came to a door next to the entrance of a leaving-shop[7].

"This is where you should come on Monday next," said Mr. Warren. "You and your friends come and say that you were invited by Mr. Warren. And they'll give you bread and butter for breakfast and hot soup for your dinner. Now, here's a penny for guiding me to the bakery, and off you go."

Ned hastened home to tell Katie. For now he had a home, if one could call it that. Katie's mother had died two months before, and Katie had kept the room. It was all she could do to earn the four shillings a week to pay the rent, but she let Ned sleep there, too. Little Emmy had become a fixture there, as her mother had far more interest in gin than in her child, and there was nowhere else for her to go—except, of course, the workhouse. The children knew that there was such a place as the workhouse, but they shrank from the very idea of it. It was a grim place: the food was poor, the inmates were separated from their families, the work which they had to do was hard and pointless, and they had to wear prison-like uniforms. And worst of all, they lost their freedom. Many of the poor preferred death to life in a workhouse. The children did not even consider taking the charity which was meted out in so ruthless a fashion.

"Ah, you're back, Neddy," said Katie, putting down the collar that she had just finished button-holing. "There weren't no water this morning and they might ha' fixed it by now. You watch Emmy while I

---

[7] leaving shop = pawn shop

go, there's a good lad." Katie grabbed the water basin and hurried out to the stand-pipe[8].

Emmy was sitting on the floor, rolling Katie's empty thread spools back and forth. Ned sat down beside Emmy and made a little stack of spools for her to knock down. He always sat on the floor, for the room boasted only one chair—the stool that Katie sat on to work. In fact, that stool was the only piece of furniture in the room. Everything else had been sold long ago to get the money for the rent.

"I got a penny," said Ned to the toddler as she giggled over the fun of knocking down the stack of spools, "and it'll buy you somethin' to eat. And you can come to school with me next week an' get breakfast *and* dinner."

Katie came back an hour later with the information that the water had never come on at all, and she had had to get some from the big tub in the yard. Ned got up to fill the mug they all shared, for he was thirsty. But after he looked at the water in the mug, he quickly poured it back into the basin.

"Mr. Hardy has been washin' his potatoes in it again," said Katie, "so it's all mucky. But if we let the water alone for a bit, the dirt'll settle on the bottom and the water on top will be all right to drink."

Katie sat down on her stool and threaded her needle.

"A gentleman bought me *two* muffins," said Ned, "an' I got a penny. What should I get for you and Emmy?"

"Better get some hot potatoes," said Katie without looking up. "It's cold enough in here. Get 'em from Mr. Hardy—we know his are clean, anyway," she added with a faint smile.

"I know a place where we can all get food next week," said Ned. "The gentleman told me to come to the Ragged School in Bethnal

---

[8] Stand-pipe = an outdoor tap that was shared by the houses in the area

Green an' they'll give us bread and butter for breakfast an' hot soup for dinner."

"But Neddy, you'd have to go to school there to get the food."

"I know. We could all go to school—you an' me an' Emmy an' Jack. We wouldn't need to work much if we was getting' the food for free."

Katie sighed impatiently. "If I don't work all day, Neddy, there'll be no shillings for the rent and we'll lose the room. And Emmy's too little to go to school."

"Oh," said Ned.

"But you and Jack go. You'll get some food and it'll be warmer there. Go on now and get the potatoes—Emmy, don't fuss. Neddy'll get you some food. Put her on the bed before you go, Ned."

Ned took the child by the hand and led her over to the pile of rags that did duty for a bed. "Wait there, Emmy," he said. "I'll be back in a minute."

All the time that Ned was gone, Katie sewed buttonholes. When he came back with the potatoes she ate one and helped Emmy to eat, and then she went back to sewing. Ned went out again to look for more parcels to carry, and Emmy lay down on the rags and slept, and Katie kept on button-holing. Emmy woke up and amused herself by playing with the pieces of wallpaper that had peeled off the damp walls, tearing them into little bits as Katie drew the needle in and out, in and out of the cloth. Katie lit the candle at five-thirty, for it was growing dark, and the light that came in at the uncurtained window was fading. By the dim light of the candle she could see just enough to keep sewing. Ned came back soon afterwards, half frozen, but having earned a brown and spent it on two oranges. These were divided between the children and eaten slowly, and then Katie wrapped her shawl around her shoulders and went on button-holing. Jack came to ask if he could sleep there and offered a penny for the privilege.

"You keep your penny, Jack," said Katie, snipping off the thread and reaching for a fresh collar, "An' buy somethin' to eat with it. You can sleep alongside Ned. You'll keep each other warm."

The boys played with Emmy and the spools for a little while, and Ned told Jack about the free food at the Ragged School. Then they curled up next to each other on Ned's pile of rags and fell asleep with the candle still lit and Katie's needle still going in and out, in and out, in and out.

Chapter 5

Bethnal Green, London

It was a raw and bitter Monday morning when Mr. Cox came to unlock the door of the Derbyshire Street Ragged School. Two boys were sitting on the pavement next to the door, and when Mr. Cox pulled out his key, they both got to their feet.

"Please, sir," said one of them, "Are you the master? Mr. Warren said we might come."

"Yes, I am Mr. Cox, the master. You are a little beforetime, but that is better than being late. And you need a wash. Come along."

He opened the door and went up a long stairway with the boys following behind. At the top of the stairs was another door; he opened it and led them into a small room. In the room there were two tables and one of these held three washing basins with empty pitchers beside them.

Mr. Cox took two of the pitchers and went down the stairs again, returning in a few moments with the pitchers full of water. He poured the water from one of them into a basin.

"There now," he said. "Here is soap and here is water and here is a towel. Wash yourselves as well as you can while I make arrangements about the food." And he took the two empty pitchers and disappeared down the stairs again.

Ned and Jack looked at the soap and the water.

"What do you do with the soap?" Ned asked.

"You rub it on yerself," said Jack. "Missus McGinty cleaned me all up once, and that's what she did. Like this." Jack put his hands into the water and then rubbed the palms of his hands over the soap. And then he swished his hands about in the water again and rubbed them on the towel.

That looked easy enough. Ned did the same. When Mr. Cox came back they held out their hands for an inspection. Mr. Cox sighed. It was not that he had never encountered such grubby children, for he had seen dozens of such in the five years he had been master at the school. It was only that it was such a busy morning for him to have to teach them how to wash. But as quickly as he could, he washed their faces, arms, necks and feet, and was tempted to invite them to his own lodgings after school for a full bath. But he did not. Who knew how many new children might come, now that food was being provided? The school was small, with few resources, and what would they do if dozens of street children appeared? It would be difficult enough to find slates for all of them without taking on the responsibility of bathing them all. A sudden vision of what his landlady's expression would be if he brought two dozen filthy urchins home with him made him smile.

When Ned and Jack were relatively clean, Mr. Cox sent them into the schoolroom to wait for him, and he went down the stairs again. The boys were beginning to think that the price of the free food was rather high. The indignity of being scrubbed and the formidable thought of "lessons" were almost enough to make them disappear down the staircase themselves. But the schoolroom was warmer than Katie's room and much warmer than the street, and now they could smell the aroma of fresh-baked bread as the baker's boy delivered it to the little ante-room where the wash-basins were.

There was evidently a woman in that room now, for the boys could hear her say, "I'll just slice and butter it and put it on these trays, shall I?"

"Yes, thank you, Miss Baillie," said the voice of Mr. Cox. "There are two new boys already in the schoolroom."

The woman appeared in the doorway of the schoolroom. She was perhaps thirty years old and plainly dressed, but with a kind and welcoming face.

"Good morning, boys," she said with a smile, "You may sit down at a desk." And she vanished into the wash-room again.

The schoolroom was filled with wide desks which had lids that could lift up to reveal a storage space underneath. The boys sat down; two children could sit at one desk. At the front of the room stood a teacher's lectern and a blackboard with writing on it, and on the wall hung a map.

Mr. Cox came in again with a notebook.

"Now then," he said, standing at his lectern and dipping his pen in ink. "I need to know your names and ages." He looked at Jack.

"Jack Ferris," offered the boy.

"And your age?"

"Eight."

"And your parents' names?"

Jack hesitated. "I don't know me dad's name—he lit out when I were young."

"Well, then, your mother's name?"

"She was Jane Ferris."

"No longer living?"

"She's dead, sir."

Mr. Cox nodded and wrote something down in his notebook. "Ever been to school before?"

"No, sir."

"And your name?" said Mr. Cox, turning to Ned.

"Ned, sir."

"Surname?"

"I dunno."

"And your age?"

"I dunno."

"I don't suppose you know your parents' names, either, then."

"No, sir."

"And you've not been to school?"

"No, sir."

"Well, then. You boys had best sit on this side of the room, where the infants class is taught by Miss Baillie—no, this row here; the other is the girls' row. Open the desk there and take out the slates and the slate pencils. You will use these until you can write well. You see the hole in the top of the desk? That is to hold an ink-pot. But in your desk it will hold a little pot of water for you to clean your slate with—there's a rag in the desk. You must never, *never* spit on your slate in order to clean it. Ah, I see the pupils are arriving." And he went into the little wash-room again.

"He said the infants sit 'ere," said Ned. "I might ha' brought Emmy if they let babies come."

"I *think*," said Jack, "that it's wot they call the ones as can't read yet. Missus McGinty said her Bill had been to school once and was in the infants class, an' I laughed at Bill for bein' with the babies, but she gave me a swipe 'round the ear and told me it weren't no such thing. It were only that he were new at the school."

Slowly the room filled with children. They looked at the newcomers in silence, but new children were not uncommon at the school, and they did not stare at the boys for very long.

When all the children had arrived, Mr. Cox shut the door and every child stood by his desk. Mr. Cox said, "We will sing 'Blest Be the Everlasting God.'" He hummed a note and then began singing, and the children sang with him.

Blest be the everlasting God
The Father of our Lord!
Be His abounding mercy praised
His majesty adored!

When from the dead He raised His Son,
And called Him to the sky,
He gave our souls a lively hope
That they should never die.

To an inheritance divine
He taught our hearts to rise;

'Tis uncorrupted, undefiled,
Unfading in the skies.

Saints by the power of God are kept,
Till the salvation come;
We walk by faith as strangers here,
Till Christ shall call us home.

Ned and Jack, of course, had never heard a hymn before. They stood silently while the other children sang and while the master read a Psalm and offered a short prayer. It was a completely unprecedented experience, and having hardly heard the name of God except as a curse, they did not understand much of what was said. Indeed, their thoughts were more particularly fastened on the bread waiting in the other room. The words of the Psalmist, "How long?" did really resonate within their hearts, but not with the same meaning the Psalmist gave them.

When the other children sat down, Ned and Jack sat down, too, and Miss Baillie and Mr. Cox went and got the trays piled with bread and butter. After Mr. Cox admonished the children not to start eating until the grace was sung, they walked around the desks and each child took one of the thick slices and put it on the desk in front of him. Finally all the children had their bread, and the teachers led them in singing:

Be present at our table Lord,
Be here and everywhere adored,
These mercies bless and grant that we
May feast in Paradise with Thee.

Then, at last, they were all allowed to eat. It did not take long for the food to disappear, and then they all sang again:

> We thank thee Lord for this our food
> But more because of Jesus' blood
> Let manna to our souls be given
> The manna now sent down from Heaven.

And then the lessons began. Miss Baillie first came to Ned and Jack and wrote an upper and lower-case "A" on each of their slates and told them to copy it as many times as they could. This they did while the other younger children were practicing other letters.

All morning, Ned and Jack practiced writing letters on their slates while the older children chanted their sums, repeated passages of Scripture in order to memorize them, and read aloud from their Bibles.

Then Miss Baillie said, "And now we will have our Bible lesson."

The attention of Ned and Jack began to wander almost as soon as Miss Baillie began speaking. The sound of footsteps coming up the stairs on the other side of the wall and the sound of crockery in the wash-room gave them the idea that dinner was on its way. But even aside from that distraction, they could not understand what Miss Baillie was talking about. Words they had never heard before like "spirit," "salvation," and "sacrifice" kept coming out of the teacher's mouth, and they would not have understood her lesson even if they had been paying attention. But even as Ned was wondering how big the bowls of soup would be, he heard one sentence that caught his attention.

40

"We must obey God," Miss Baillie said, "For God made us."

Ned had never wondered who made him; if he had been asked he would have replied that he was nobody's child. It was a new thought that God had had anything to do with him.

"And now we will have drill." Mr. Cox's voice broke into his thoughts. Immediately all the students put their hands by their sides.

"Clear," said Mr. Cox. The children put their books or slates on their laps.

"Lift." The children put their hands on the edges of the desk flaps.

"Desks." They raised the flaps without any noise.

"Return." The books and slates were put inside the desk.

"Close." The desk flaps were lowered silently.

"Stand." In unison, all of the pupils—except for Ned and Jack—stood to their feet.

"Out." The children moved one step out from the desk and then one step in front.

"Well done," said Mr. Cox. "Please be seated. The monitors may come to the ante-room; you other pupils stay at your desks while the soup is brought out."

When the food had been given out, the children sang the grace and then they all ate the steaming pea soup. When all were finished they sang again, and then the children sitting in one row were given the task of gathering up the empty bowls and taking them back to the wash-room. All the children then washed their hands and were sent downstairs so that the room could be "aired"—the windows being opened wide for this purpose. The children loitered on the pavement for half an hour until Mr. Cox fetched them in again. Once they had washed their hands again and were seated they had spelling, recitation, and another drill. Finally there was another hymn, prayer, and Bible reading, and at last school was over.

"An' what did you learn?" asked Katie when Ned and Jack came back.

"I dunno," said Ned. His mind was a confused jumble of letters, numbers, drills, and hymns. "They have good soup," he said. And then as an afterthought he added, "God made me."

Chapter 6

N ed and Jack were not the new children for long; news about the free food spread, and more and more children started coming to school. After two weeks the room was overflowing. The smallest children were seated three to a desk and some shared slates, but at last new children had to be turned away. Mr. Warren was a frequent visitor. He usually contrived to arrive in time for the noon meal, so that he could inform his daughters that the soup fund was fulfilling its purpose. For Ned and Jack, days settled into a routine. The morning walk to Derbyshire Street, the washing, the songs, and the drills all became habit. The strange talk about salvation, righteousness, and repentance became familiar, even if it was not really understood.

On a morning in March as Ned was practicing his alphabet on his slate, the door opened unexpectedly and Mr. Warren came in, accompanied by a ragged boy. Ned felt Jack stiffen beside him; his wide eyes were fixed on the boy. Ned could interpret these signs—they meant that the new boy was a bully. The older students were working in their copybooks, and after quick glances at the intruders they went back to copying the words on the pages before them. Mr. Cox went into the ante-room with Mr. Warren and the boy, but Ned could still make out some of the words in their conversation.

"Sorry to intrude...most anxious that Frank have an opportunity...hearing by chance that George Pate will not be returning...family now in Westminster...thought I would bring him before another took the place..."

And Mr. Cox's voice replying "...George definitely not returning...Frank may have the place... must wash first...thank you, Mr. Warren...good morning..."

Boy and master returned to the classroom, and Mr. Cox said, "Frank, you may sit there in the empty seat by Harry." Harry was about eleven years old, but even he wriggled a little in his seat at the thought of Frank the Basher sitting next to him. Frank looked to be about ten, but his swaggering walk was like that of an old tough. He had evidently been at school before. At least, he seemed to know what to do with a pen and a copybook.

After half an hour, the slates and copybooks were put away and arithmetic lessons were begun. In unison the younger children chanted, "One and one is two, two and one is three, three and one is four..." and Ned and Jack knew enough now to join in most of the chanting. When this was finished, Miss Baillie's pupils worked sums on their slates while the older students listened to Mr. Cox explain something about "fractions," using the blackboard. Ned stole a look at Frank. He was not paying attention.

After the mid-day soup, the children all went downstairs while the windows were opened. The children spread out along the road, talking in little knots or looking into the windows of the shops. Some

of the boys chased each other. It was a cold day even for March, and
Ned and Jack stood together in front of the leaving-shop window,
which displayed a battered chair, a teapot, and an old peacoat.

"Who's Frank?" asked Ned.

"He's a bad lot," said Jack. "I hope 'e ain't diddling Mr. Warren."

"How do you mean?"

"He pulled a dodge on the vicar of St. Phillip's—'e were a regular
groaner."

"Groaner?"

"Goes along to meetings an' sighs an' groans about being a poor
wretch as is doomed for 'is sins. And then when the good people have
had a whip-round[9] to help the poor lad and set 'im on the right path,
he picks the pockets of them as is in the church pew with 'im. I think
he made off with a prayer-book, too." His sentence ended in a cough.

Across the street from the boys was a coster with a donkey and
cart, selling oranges. "Oranges!" boomed the coster. "Fresh, sweet
oranges! Three-a-penny! Only a penny for three fresh, sweet oranges!"

"I ain't seen him before," said Ned.

"That's Boxer Bill," said Jack. "'e's usually at Coventry Street."

"I want to see that donkey," said Ned. Costers with donkeys were
rare in Ned's neighbourhood. The boys crossed the road and stood on
the pavement looking at the donkey. He was a patient, sleepy little
creature that took not the slightest notice of his master's "patter" or
the boys staring so curiously at him. Ned noticed Frank crossing the
street, and his heart sank as the boy looked intently at him and gave
an unpleasant grin. However, instead of saying anything, Frank turned
to the donkey. After a sidelong glance at the donkey's owner, he
quickly untied one of the ropes that were used as a harness. Stepping

---

[9] had a whip-round = to take up a collection

back suddenly, he grabbed Ned's arm and shouted, "'Ere! I catched 'im! Mister!"

The coster's quick ear caught the words and he stopped his patter in mid-sentence. He strode hastily around to where the boys were.

"Wot's all this?"

"'E did somethin' to yer donkey ropes—I seen 'im!"

The coster glanced at the dangling rope. "Beggar brat!" he roared. "For a farthing I'd lather you!" The coster raised a massive hand and cuffed Ned on the ear. "That'll learn you to mess with my donkey! Now hook it!" Ned would not cry, although the whole side of his face ached. He backed away as the coster, still muttering, bent to re-tie the rope. While the eyes of the street were directed to this exchange, Frank stealthily helped himself to an orange.

When school was over for the day, Ned and Jack, who had begun sniffling and coughing more and more frequently throughout the afternoon, went to the train station to see if they could carry any parcels. It was a good day for them; they each earned a half-penny, and the exercise of walking swiftly warmed them up a bit. As they walked back to Katie's room, they passed a youth with a tray of oranges calling, "Four-a-penny! Best sweet oranges! Four for one penny! Plump and juicy!"

"Let's get some oranges," said Jack, who had been wanting one ever since the incident with the coster. "They're goin' cheap." They purchased the oranges and carried them back to Katie and Emmy. But as they entered the room, they were surprised to see that Katie was not sewing. She was sitting on her stool, crying.

"Wot's wrong?" asked Ned.

Katie gave a helpless little shrug, making no effort to wipe away the tears coursing down her cheeks. "The landlord said he's raisin' the rent to five shillin' a week. I told him I couldn't pay it and he said there's those that will. So we're out the room."

"Oh." said Ned. The boys stood silent; the only sound was that of Emmy rolling empty thread spools along the floor.

"It don't matter for me," said Jack after a moment. "It ain't so cold now. Ned an' I will doss[10] where we can."

Katie gave a long, shuddering sigh. No, the boys wouldn't mind so much. They had been used to sleeping on the streets. And they couldn't know what it would mean for her and for Emmy to lose the room. Without a room, how could she make button-holes? And without that work, how would they eat?

""Ere's some oranges," said Ned, offering her one.

Without enthusiasm, Katie took it. She thought she might as well feed Emmy. But almost as soon as she began peeling it, she stopped.

"It's boiled," she said.

"Boiled?" said Jack with a cough.

"When the oranges get old an' wrinkled, some costers boil 'em to make 'em look plump an' shiny. But they don't taste right an' they go off after a day." She spoke listlessly and let the orange fall to the floor. Emmy toddled over to pick up the orange and suck on it. The boys shuffled their feet uncomfortably.

"I'll be off to work, then," said Ned, looking away. "I'll get somethin' else fer us to eat." He went out, followed by Jack. The two boys said nothing to each other—what was there to say?—and parted to look for work.

---

[10] doss = have a place to sleep

Ned hurried down Club Street toward the train station. He had been looking forward to an orange, and hoped he might earn enough to buy one after all.

"Ned!"

He stopped and looked across the street to find out who had called him. The man waved and beckoned him to cross. It was Toyman Tim, so called because he sold penny toys on the streets.

"Need a job?" said Toyman when Ned reached him. "I gots an order for all the toys I can bring—big children's party in Holloway. I can only carry one tray, but if you can get the other...Good! They ain't too heavy. Lemme get that strap shorter around yer neck. All right. Look sharp! It's a goodish stretch." Toyman led the way and Ned trotted behind. "I were doin' my usual streets an' not selling much, so I went further out to Holloway, and still weren't selling much, when out comes a lady from her house and sees me and says, 'There's a tea party for some poor children in Whitechapel tomorrow, and we want to give them some toys. Is that all you have?' And I says, 'Oh, no, missus, I have twice this many at home.' And she says, 'If you can be back in two hours with the rest I'll buy them all.' Ain't it a stroke of luck!" Ned agreed, and hoped that Toyman's good humour at this unexpected large sale would prompt him to be generous when paying his helper.

He was. When the lady had bought all the toys and given Toyman his money, he gave Ned two pence. As they were walking back to Shoreditch, Ned saw the perfect place to spend the night. He would return here when it was dark. When he reached his own neighbourhood, Ned bought oranges with one penny and some fried fish with the other. He put the oranges into his shirt carried the fish in his hands and took it all back to Katie's room. She was still there, only she had stopped crying and had begun button-holing again. She greeted him with a half-smile.

"Paper Poll upstairs says Emmy an' me can doss with her for a few nights anyway. If Emmy won't tear her papers." She looked worriedly at the child, who was tearing more wallpaper from the walls. "Paper Poll" was an artificial flower maker who used coloured tissue paper to create her blooms. Ned didn't see how Katie would keep Emmy from touching those papers, especially while she was buttonholing, but he said nothing.

They ate the food that Ned had brought and then Ned helped Katie by carrying the stool up to Paper Poll's room. Katie followed with Emmy. The stairwell was dark. There were several stairs missing, and the handrail had long ago disappeared. Even so, Ned only stumbled once. They reached Poll's door and knocked.

"Come in," said Poll's voice, and Ned opened the door.

Poll was a woman whose age was hard to guess—she might have been anything between thirty and fifty. She had a table and a chair and was sitting there now with her small, sharp scissors, cutting the papers into the shapes she needed. Around the room were boxes of already finished flowers in all colours, giving the room a cheerful air. Poll's face, however, was anything but cheerful as she looked at Ned.

"He ain't stayin' too, is he?"

"No, he's just helpin' me," said Katie. "Put the stool over there, Neddy, where there's a space." Ned put down the stool and then nodded a goodbye to Katie. She patted his head as he passed. He went out to find Jack. This took a couple of hours, as Jack had found an errand to run that had taken him to Stepney. But at last he appeared at Mr. Abel's pie shop, and Ned waited while he ate.

"I found a good place to sleep tonight," Ned said quietly. "In Holloway. I'll show you when it's dark." And so the two boys lingered around the streets until darkness was well established, and then they started off for Holloway.

Chapter 7

The policeman was lost in his thoughts as he walked his beat down Wellington Street at eleven o'clock that night. The light drizzle and chill wind were unpleasant, but he was used to them. His contemplations centred on his wages, and what could be done to improve them. As a new policeman, his wages were twenty shillings a week, but if his review was satisfactory, his pay would rise to twenty-two shillings. Not that it mattered for himself, but he wanted to get married. And Miss Elmsworth's father would not think twenty shillings a week was sufficient to support his daughter. He knew within his heart that twenty-two shillings would probably not be considered sufficient, either, but he could not help hoping. Eventually he might make as much as twenty-six shillings a week before being promoted to a first class sergeant (as of course he would), earning the princely sum of thirty-one shillings a week. So busy was he calculating how long it would take him to arrive at that level of income, and how soon he might broach the topic with Mr. Elmsworth, that it took several seconds for him to realize that he had heard the sound of a rasping cough. He stopped walking and listened. Another cough. It seemed to be coming from the alleyway he had just passed.

Could there be some urchins sleeping back there? There were not many "street arabs" in Holloway, it being a better neighbourhood than places like Bethnal Green. But these sorts of children could turn up almost anywhere. The alley ran alongside a baker's shop, and the heat from the ovens kept the bricks of the back wall of the bakery warm for many hours into the night. It was the sort of place that street children looked for. The policeman was not a cruel man, but he suffered from a limited imagination. It did not occur to him to wonder where boys were to go at night if they had no home. All he knew was that no one was allowed to sleep out of doors. His duty then was to take them along to the police station and charge them with vagrancy. Some policemen merely moved the boys along, but he wanted to do everything properly in order to give himself the best possible chance of promotion. He moved quietly into the alley, keeping his bulls-eye[11] off until he came up to a huddled lump. Then he shined his light at it and saw newspapers spread over something. He swept them aside and found two boys sleeping huddled next to the warm wall.

"All right, let's be having you out!" said the policeman. "No sleeping here!" The boys, suddenly roused with a strong grip on their arms made a little struggle, but soon subsided. The policeman led them out to the pavement and looked at them sternly. Jack coughed again. "Now, lads, you know you mustn't sleep out of doors. You will go before the magistrate and we'll see what he says."

Taking each boy by one arm, the policeman began to move off toward the police station. There would be no chance of escape, Ned

---

[11] bulls-eye = an early version of a flashlight (called a "torch" in Britain)

thought, unless the policeman happened to see a burglar and had to give chase. But there seemed little hope of that.

It was a bitter night, and the street was deserted. No, not quite deserted—there was one man walking towards them. A glance showed that he was obviously not a desperate criminal; he had an umbrella and a good coat and hat. The man drew closer and then a slightly familiar voice said, "Ned? Is that you?"

"Mr. Warren?" said Ned.

"You know them, sir?" asked the policeman.

"I do. What's the trouble?"

"Vagrancy. Sleeping out of doors. They'll have to go before the magistrate."

There was a pause, during which Jack gave another rasping cough, and then Mr. Warren said, "I'll take them, if you please. I give you my word that you will not find them sleeping out of doors again."

"Will you? Very good, sir," said the policeman. He let go of the boys, tipped his hat to Mr. Warren, and moved away to continue walking his beat.

"Now then, Ned and —Jack, isn't it? Yes. Well now, lads, what is it you're doing sleeping here?"

"We lost the room, sir. Katie and Emmy can doss with Paper Poll for a few days, but we ain't got a room."

"But what are you doing all this way from Shoreditch?"

"Well, sir, I was doin' a job with Toyman Tim today an' saw the bakery an' thought that there wouldn't be any other boys tryin' to sleep there...not in Holloway, sir."

"Hmm," said Mr. Warren. He had been sorrowful even before he saw the boys; he had been called out to attend the deathbed of a member of his congregation and it seemed just now that tragedy met him wherever he went. He looked at the boys in the pale gaslight. Tired and tousled, they looked smaller than ever. Jack coughed again.

"I know a place where you can stay," said Mr. Warren, "But it's a good distance from here. We'll get a cab." Together they walked to the cab-stand, and got into a cab. "Stepney," said Mr. Warren to the driver. "Barnardo's Boys Home." The boys had never been in a cab before and would have found the experience thrilling if they had not known that the loss of their freedom was the price they were paying for it.

The cab pulled up at 17 Stepney Causeway. Mr. Warren and the boys got out and Mr. Warren asked the driver to wait. It was a large building, and Mr. Warren knocked loudly on the door. It was answered almost immediately by a young man who peered at them for a moment and then without a word opened the door wide and let them in. It was a dangerous district, and it was not wise to have lingering conversations on doorsteps in the middle of the night. He ushered them into a small office where a light was already burning. An open book on the desk showed that he had been reading.

"Good evening, sir," he said, shaking hands with Mr. Warren. "May I help you?"

"I am Thomas Warren, the Baptist minister in Holloway. This is Jack, and this is Ned. They have no home and no family. They were being taken in by a policeman for sleeping out of doors when I offered to bring them here. May they stay?"

The young man nodded. "Of course. As you know, no really needy child is ever turned away. Do you know these boys personally, or have you just met them this evening?"

"I have known them for several months. They attend a Ragged School in Bethnal Green which I have some connection with. For some little time they had a room to sleep in, shared with other children, but they have all been turned out of it."

"And where are the other children?"

"Both girls. They are lodging with a neighbour temporarily, but I don't know where they will go after that. One is an infant, I understand."

"They might go to the Girls Village," said the young man thoughtfully. "Perhaps you will call again and we can look into it. Now, however, we must see about getting these boys a bed for the night."

Mr. Warren gave each boy a pat on the back and promised that he would visit them in a few days. He shook the young man's hand and went back outside to the waiting cab. They watched him go with anxious eyes.

"Follow me, boys," said the young man. "I am Mr. Slater. It is too late this evening to admit you properly—that can be done tomorrow." He picked up a lighted candle in its holder and led them down a hallway, up a staircase, down another hallway and into a small room. From a chest of drawers he took two nightshirts and gave them to the boys. "You ought to wash first, but it is very late. We will attend to it in the morning. Please take your clothes off, and put these on instead." It did not take the boys long to get undressed. The damp rags that they had been wearing constantly for months fell off them with very little persuasion, and the clean, dry nightshirts were quickly substituted. When this had been done, the boys followed Mr. Slater to another room where ten beds were lined up next to each other.

"One of you sleep here," whispered the man, pointing to a bed, "And the other sleep in that bed there." Ned got into bed and the man pulled a blanket up over him. He did the same for Jack, and then whispered, "Good night." The candle moved out of the room and the light and the footsteps faded down the hall together.

Ned was bewildered. Never in his life had he slept on a mattress or a pillow, and rarely had he had a proper blanket—certainly not one which smelled so clean. He could hear the other boys breathing. Once or twice Jack coughed. There was just enough moonlight coming in the window that he could dimly see the row of beds, each with a lump of boy on it. He lay there perfectly still. His ear was still sore from the swipe he had got from Boxer Bill that afternoon. An hour ago—was it only an hour ago?—he had been huddled beneath a newspaper, sleeping outdoors on a wet night. And yet here he was, warm and dry and lying on the softest thing he could imagine. It was so unlike what he was used to that it frightened him. He could not even see these new surroundings properly in the dark. A feeling of panic began to creep over him. What was this place—was it like the workhouse? Perhaps he could sneak back out of the building and escape onto the street. But it was so dark, and he wasn't sure of the way out...and then the words of a hymn they sang at school came to his mind unbidden:

> Though it be the gloom of night,
> Though we see no ray of light,
> Since the Lord Himself is there
> 'Tis not meet that we should fear.
>
> Night with Him is never night;
> Where He is, there all is light;
> When He calls us, why delay?
> They are happy who obey.

Ned had sung those words many times without even thinking of what they meant, but now he seemed to understand them. *"Since the Lord Himself is there..."* Here? In the dark? *"Night with Him is never night..."* Somehow, the thought was comforting. The fear which had started to take hold of him began to subside, and a feeling of peace took its place. He yawned and turned onto his side. Perhaps staying here one night would be all right. He could always run away tomorrow night. His eyes closed, and he joined the others in sleep.

Chapter 8

At six o'clock the next morning, the sound of a bell clanging nearly above his head woke Ned from his deep sleep. Accustomed to waken at the slightest noise, Ned jumped out of bed immediately, before he could even remember where he was. It was still dark outside, but the lights were lit and Ned could see the other boys crawling out of their beds and beginning to dress.

A different man, not Mr. Slater, was standing by the door. He must have been the one who rang the bell, Ned thought. He held a piece of paper in his hand and he looked from it to Ned and Jack.

"Good morning, boys," he said. "I am Mr. Langley. You came last night?"

"Yes, sir," said Ned. Jack coughed and nodded his head.

Mr. Langley had been on the staff of the Home for Destitute Boys for only a few days, and this was his first experience of taking new boys into the Home. He looked at Jack with concern—the cough had a nasty sound to it. Ought he to take him to the infirmary to see the doctor right away? No, he probably should get him washed and dressed and properly inducted into the institution first. "We'll see about that cough presently," he said. "But first you will need some clothes. Follow me." He led them to the room where they had got their nightshirts the night before and found each of them trousers, a shirt, a jacket, shoes, socks, and a cap. He made each boy's clothes into a little pile and had them carry their new garments with them as he led them down to the bathroom. Here he gave them a bath—possibly the first full bath of their lives. Then they put on their new clothes. The clothes were warm but confining. To their unaccustomed feet the shoes felt rigid and uncomfortable, and they would just as soon have taken them off again.

When they were dressed they were taken in to the photograph room to have their pictures taken. In the middle of the room was the large camera pointed at a chair which was against the wall. One at a time, the boys sat in the chair while Mr. Langley put his head beneath the cloth of the camera and told them to look at the camera and hold still. He had been shown how to take a photograph only the day before, and he hoped he was doing it correctly. Then Mr. Langley took them down another hallway, and knocked on a closed door.

"Enter," said a voice within, and Mr. Langley opened the door and ushered them into an office. The man sitting behind the desk rose to meet them.

"Good morning, sir," said Mr. Langley. "This is Ned, and this is Jack. They came in very late last night, brought by a Mr. Warren of Holloway. Here is Slater's report—very brief, as it was so late."

The man, who was tall and thin, shook the boys' hands and said, "I am Mr. Appleton, the Resident Master of the home. Mr. Langley, have these boys had anything to eat since they arrived?"

"No, sir."

"Then, if you please, will you be certain there is food waiting for them in the dining room when I have finished talking with them? Thank you. And will you send a messenger boy to bring them to the dining room in half an hour? Thank you, Mr. Langley."

Mr. Langley left the room and Mr. Appleton placed two chairs in front of the desk and bid them be seated. He sat down at his desk and looked at the report, then took a pen in his hand and asked for their histories. It did not take long to tell him all they knew. Jack knew a little more than Ned, of course, and between coughs gave what account he could of himself. All Ned knew was that he had appeared in Button-hole Row as a toddler, and no one had ever claimed him. He was not even sure who had named him Ned.

"Well," said Mr. Appleton, "You must have a surname. I will have to give you one. Let me see...." Ned waited while Mr. Appleton thought for a moment. "Harrison. I think that will do. Ned Harrison...Edward Harrison...a fine-sounding name. But we'll continue to call you Ned for everyday." He wrote the name down on his papers. "And we must give you an age." He looked at Ned with a practiced eye. "We'll say you're seven. You're near enough that, I suppose. Now then, the notes here say that you've both attended school. Is that correct? Good. Tomorrow you will start classes here. Ah, here is Dick. Dick, will you please take Ned here to the dining room? There is some food set aside for him. Jack, I believe I will take you to the infirmary myself and have some food brought there for you. I would like Dr. Milne to look at you; you seem to be feverish."

The boy Dick had a friendly face. He was about nine years old and was wearing the same clothes as Ned and Jack. In fact, all the boys wore the same clothes.

"You're new, ain't you?" said Dick as he walked with Ned to the dining room. Ned nodded. "I saw you this morning in our room. How do you like the clothes? A bit stiff at first, but warm, eh? You'll get used to 'em. That door leads to the workshops. You'll learn a trade while you're here. I'm with the shoes. Maybe I worked on the shoes you're wearing."

"Is it...is it a workhouse, then?" asked Ned quietly.

"This place? Nothin' like it. You never been in a workhouse, have yer? Thought not. I was in one once. Wasn't it the horrors! The workhouse gives yer just a bit of everythin'—a bit o' food, a bit o' schoolin', a bit o' religion, but only 'cause they has to and you gets the worst of it all. The stairs to the schoolroom are over there," he added, pointing.

"I thought you had to work in a workhouse," ventured Ned.

"Work? Well, they keeps you busy. I had to take ropes apart for the oakum. You don't learn nothin' that helps you earn a living when you get out of the workhouse. Now in this home, we *work*, but it ain't a punishment. You'll see. Here's the dining room."

Two bowls of porridge were set out on a table, and Ned sat down and picked up a spoon. He hoped that Dick would stay with him. He did not much like the idea of eating alone in such a large, silent room. By way of retaining his companion, he said, "So if it ain't a workhouse, what is it?"

"It's Barnardo's home for boys; didn't you know that?"

Ned shook his head. "Who's Barnardo?"

Dick sat down next to Ned. "He's the man as started it. He comes visitin' sometimes."

"How long have you been here?"

Dick's forehead wrinkled as he thought. "Near on two years."

"Who brought you?"

"Bible Braidy."

"Who?"

"Bible Braidy. I dunno what 'is real name is, but he were a good bloke. Always helpin' out the poor folk and telling them about the way to heaven. He could tell yer everything about the Bible. He kept an eye out for all the little 'uns and gave us a brown now and then—though he weren't over-rich himself. Me dad weren't much good to us—always boozy and like as not to give us a kick or a slogg. And then he were sent to prison, and we was near starvin', so one day Bible Braidy he takes us and brings us here."

"Your mum didn't care?"

"Mum's dead. Popped off when we were little."

"We? You have a brother?"

"No, no brothers. Two sisters."

"And they're here?

"Not to say *here*. They're at the Girls Village."

Ned remembered hearing something about a girls village last night. "What's that?"

"Oh, it's like to this place, but there's a bunch o' little houses instead of one big house. There's a lady in each house as takes care of the girls."

Ned only nodded, but he was thinking of Katie and Emmy. He would like it if Emmy could have some of this porridge. He finished his bowl, hesitated, and then ate the other bowl as well. When all the food was gone, the boys stayed where they were, talking: Ned did not know where to go, and Dick was evidently only too willing to trade the boredom of the messenger-boys' room for an interesting chat with a newcomer. Mr. Appleton, meanwhile, had returned to his office and was talking to Mr. Langley.

"These two new boys slept in your dormitory last night, did they not? I think they should remain there, as those beds were empty. That is to say, Ned should remain there. Dr. Milne has seen the boy Jack. He's afraid he's settling in for pneumonia, so he will be in the infirmary until he recovers." He did not say, "If he recovers," though both men knew that Jack might die. Undernourished eight year olds were not adept at surviving pneumonia.

"What shall I do with Ned now, sir? Do new boys fall in step with all their duties immediately? Shall I take him to the schoolroom?"

Mr. Appleton glanced at the clock on the wall. "No, school time is half over; it would be difficult for the master to accommodate a new boy now. Perhaps you could take him to the dormitory and teach him how to make his bed. From his account of himself, he has never had a bed. You might also show him how to wash himself so that he will know what to do tomorrow morning, and then take him around the building and let him see the various departments. Then it will be dinner time and he may join the other children for the rest of the day. It was Dick Lenkin that took him to the breakfast room, wasn't it? And he is in your dormitory as well, I think. Good, he's a gregarious sort; he'll help him settle in and help him with learning some of the work."

"And what trade shall he be put in?"

"I believe more help is needed in the bakery. Take him there personally after housework and introduce him to the master there. For the rest, he will follow what the other boys do, and they will help to teach him what his duties are."

"I see, sir. Thank you."

"Very well, then, Mr. Langley. Good morning."

Mr. Langley found Ned and Dick in the dining room.

"Dick, you may go back to the messenger-boys room. Ned, take your bowls and bring them over to the table there, beside the door that leads to the kitchen. When it is your turn to wait tables, this is where the dirty plates will go."

"Sir," said Ned, "Did Jack get 'is food?"

"Yes, your friend Jack had a good meal in the infirmary. The doctor would like him to remain there for a little while, so that he can help him to feel better. But you will stay in the room you were in last night. Now, come with me to the dormitory. I will teach you how to make a bed."

Ned followed Mr. Langley down corridors and up stairs that were beginning to look slightly familiar. When they reached the room, eight of the beds were neatly made. Jack's and Ned's had the sheets stripped off the mattresses to be washed (the boys had been put into bed quite dirty the night before), but clean linens and blankets were folded neatly on the mattresses. Mr. Langley made Ned's bed, telling Ned to watch carefully. Then the sheets and blankets were tousled, and Ned was allowed to try to make his own bed. The first attempt was not very good, so Mr. Langley made it one more time, tousled it again, and gave Ned another chance. This time Ned did better. Mr. Langley praised him and said that in a few days he would be able to make his bed as well as Dick made his. Then he showed Ned the wooden box with a hinged lid that was stowed under the bed. In the box was a clean nightshirt and another change of clothes exactly like the ones he had on.

"This is where you will keep the clothes that you are not wearing," said Mr. Langley. "Once a week you will go to the laundry-room with the other boys and wash your clothes and sheets. You see, teaching you boys to do the laundry, cleaning, baking, cooking, shoemaking and so forth not only teaches you skills that will serve you the whole of your life, but also cuts the cost of running the Home. Now, I will take you to the bathroom and show you how you will wash yourself every morning and evening. After that I can show you around the building, and then it will be time to eat. You had a big breakfast not long ago; will you be hungry enough to eat a little lunch?"

Ned's eager nod made him chuckle, and he led the way to the bathroom.

Chapter 9

By the evening of the second full day of life in the Home, Ned was exhausted. Always before, he had worked until he had earned enough to eat something, and then he was free to wander the streets looking for amusement. But in this place, every moment of his time was organized.

At six o'clock the boys were awakened with a bell. They dressed, washed, made their beds, and then went to the dining room for morning prayers and breakfast. Next, unless it was their turn to be messengers or to help fix the dinner, came several hours in the schoolroom, a large, airy room at the top of the building. The boys sat at desks like the ones Ned had used at the Ragged School, and four different teachers taught the different sections of boys. Then came the mid-day meal: a hot dinner that tasted good and filled him up. This was followed by housework, a different chore every day. That day's chore had been to scrub the schoolroom floor. Twenty boys with their shoes and stockings off and trousers rolled up to their knees had knelt in a line with their brushes and buckets full of soapy water and scrubbed their way across the floor. On other days, Dick told him, they would do their laundry, help prepare food, or clean the bathroom. Then each boy went to his trade: some to shoemaking, some to baking, others to learn the work of carpenters, engineers, or tailors. After that came physical drill and games—rounders was the game they had played that day. Finally, supper came; then there was the work of clearing the dishes. Dick told him that the next day it would be their dormitory's turn to help with the washing up. At last there was a little time when the boys could choose their own activities. Many elected to read books they had borrowed from the bookcases in the schoolroom. Other boys played with marbles or practiced their musical instruments, for the Home had its own marching band. A few boys had pen-knives with which they whittled toys or whistles. Evening prayers and preparation for bed followed this, and then at ten o'clock the lights went out.

As Ned had been on his knees scrubbing, surrounded by water and soapsuds, he had very nearly decided to escape that night. The temptation was a little diminished by the good food at supper, and the friendliness of Dick over a game of marbles weakened it even further. By the time he was curled up on his clean, soft bed, he was too tired to do anything but close his eyes.

The next morning Mr. Langley appeared in the school room and summoned Ned to come with him. As they went down the stairs, he told Ned that there was a visitor come to see him.

"Mr. Warren?" asked Ned, and Mr. Langley nodded. Ned's face, which was usually impassive, broke into a smile.

He's really an attractive little chap when he smiles like that, thought Mr. Langley. *He's usually so silent and retiring that I've hardly got a smile or word out of him. He doesn't fight against the rules, he puts his heart into whatever work he's doing, and he is respectful. But for all that I doubt whether he is converted. He doesn't seem to pay attention much during prayers.*

A small room near the front entrance to the building was known as the reception room. Some of the boys had parents who came to visit them occasionally, and this room, furnished with a few chairs, was the room where such meetings took place. Mr. Warren was waiting there, and when Ned entered he shook the boy's hand and clapped him on the back. Ned grinned at Mr. Warren. Never in his life could he remember anyone seeking him out.

"Don't you look smart in those clothes!" said Mr. Warren admiringly. "Are you getting on all right?"

"Yes, sir."

"Feeding you well, are they?"

"Oh, yes sir!" said Ned with such energy that Mr. Warren laughed.

"I'm glad to hear it. Well, I promised I would come to see how you boys were faring, and I can see that you're well."

"Jack's not very well, sir. He's in a 'fermery,' they said."

"Ah, yes," said Mr. Warren. "They told me that Jack is in the infirmary. I'll go and see him in a moment."

Ned had hardly asked a favour of anyone in all his seven years, but he made bold to ask one now.

"Sir, do you think Emmy an' Katie could go to that village for girls? I don't know as Paper Poll will let 'em stay with her for long, and there's nowheres else for 'em to go. They'd get food an' beds an' everything at that village."

Mr. Warren reached out his hand and put it on Ned's shoulder. "One of the reasons I came today was to see what needed to be done to get them into the Girls Village. I will go and find them as soon as I leave here and bring both to Ilford. Where does Paper Poll live?"

"Nichols Street, sir. Number eighteen, upstairs. Thank you, sir."

"All right, Ned," said Mr. Langley. "You may tell Mr. Warren goodbye, and then you are dismissed to go back to the schoolroom."

"Goodbye, sir," said Ned, holding out his hand, "And thank you *very much.*"

"Goodbye, Ned," said Mr. Warren, and watched the boy out of the room. "He's a plucky fellow," he said to Mr. Langley. "I met him when he carried a box of books for me last summer. I knew he would make good if he went to school."

"Yes, he seems to be a fine lad, though he is very quiet. He heard the gospel, I'm sure, at the Ragged School?"

"Oh, yes, he must have. I do not know if he has ever responded to it, however. It often takes a long time, you know, Mr. Langley, for these children to understand the gospel, and even then they might not believe—like adults, as I dare say you know."

"Yes. Before I came here, I worked with the George Yard Mission, teaching Bible classes to the men."

"You don't teach the boys here in exactly the same way, I trust."

"Oh, no. The boys wouldn't stick it for one thing," said Mr. Langley, lapsing for a moment into the slang of his charges. "We have prayers morning and evening, a weekly Bible lesson, and a Sunday service, but none of them are lengthy, and the simplest language is used. And of course I put in a word to the boys when I can. I understand that many boys have been converted by this means, and I'm sure many more will in time. I have been here only a week myself, Mr. Warren, but the salvation of these boys is an anxious thing for me.

The words of the apostle keep coming to my mind: 'We pray you in Christ's stead, be ye reconciled to God.'"

"If that is your heart's cry, Mr. Langley, the boys could not wish for a better guide than you will be. I believe you will soon see fruit from your labours." He picked up his hat from the chair he had laid it on and shook Mr. Langley's hand goodbye. "I will go and see the boy Jack in the infirmary. Is he very poorly?"

"I believe he has developed pneumonia, but he is not dangerously ill. I'm sure he would enjoy a visit from you as much as Ned has. Goodbye, Mr. Warren."

Mr. Warren's visit did indeed cheer the spirits of Jack. A private word with the doctor afterwards confirmed that though it was too early to be certain, it did seem that Jack would probably pull through.

"Brought in just in the nick of time, I think," said the doctor. "It was you who brought him here, was it not? Jack has mentioned your name to me. Well, if anyone will be able to take credit for saving his life, I think you will have the precedence. It was a good night's work. God bless you, sir."

Fortified with these encouraging words, Mr. Warren set off to find Katie and Emmy. It took him longer than he had imagined it would to find number eighteen, Nichols Street, particularly as there were three streets next to each other which all had "Nichols" in the name. At last he found the right house, made his way up the rickety and foul-smelling stairs, and gained entrance into Poll's room. Instead of his quest being at an end, however, he found that the search had only begun, and might be in vain after all. Poll informed him that as Emmy had torn up several of her paper flowers, she had told Katie that very morning that she could not stay any longer.

"It ain't my business to keep children," she said, finishing cutting out some bright yellow paper into an intricate shape and putting it down. "Katie's a good girl, I ain't sayin' she isn't, but that baby was tearin' up my stock. I has to look out fer my business. Katie oughter ha' left the baby somewheres and so I told 'er, but she wouldn't hear tell of it. I don't know where they went. You'll have a job to find 'em!"

"You've no idea at all?"

"'Ow should I know? Said she were going to take her stool to a leaving-shop and get some money for it. Now I has my work to do." Poll picked up her scissors again and took up a new sheet of bright yellow paper, indicating that the interview was over.

As Mr. Warren descended the stairs, a hopeless feeling settled over him. It seemed unlikely that he would be able to find the girls now. He did not know what they looked like or even what exact age Katie was. He supposed he could wander the streets of Shoreditch looking for a girl with a toddler on one arm and carrying a stool with the other...but no, she would have pawned the stool by now. As he stood outside the house, wondering if there was anything he could do, his attention was arrested by the sight of a girl who looked to be about twelve with a toddler on one arm and carrying a stool with the other. Amazed that she should appear just at that moment, he breathed a prayer of heartfelt thanks. The girl was coming toward him, and he could see that she looked distressed.

When she drew near enough to speak to, he said, "Pardon me, but are you Katie that was so kind to Ned and Jack?"

Katie stopped and looked at him. "I am." Her brow creased in concern. "They ain't come to harm, have they, sir?"

"No, indeed. I am Mr. Warren, who has some connection with the Ragged School they attended."

Katie's brow cleared. "I heard of you, sir, an' your kindness to the boys."

"And this is Emmy, is it?"

"Yes, this is Emmy." The child smiled at the sound of her name.

"Tell me, have you anywhere to sleep tonight?"

The look of distress came back to Katie's face. "Not yet, sir. I was hopin' to pawn my stool and get enough for some food an' a bed in a lodging-house, but the leaving-shop man said he had enough stools that couldn't be sold, an' he didn't need another. I was goin' to ask Poll if she could keep it for me till next week—I could try again then."

"But where will you sleep until then? And how will you eat?"

"I...I don't know, sir." Katie's face crumpled and the sobs she had held back bravely for many hours finally burst forth.

"There, there, my girl," said Mr. Warren kindly, "I have a plan for you and Emmy. Ned and Jack have gone to Mr. Barnardo's Home for boys. You have heard of it, have you not? Well, they have lovely food, warm beds, and good clothes. Jack is ill just now, but he has excellent medical care. And Ned is going to school and learning a trade. Now then, Ned asked me to find you and Emmy and bring you to the Girls Village in Ilford. You and Emmy could live in a cottage with some other girls and a kind lady who is like a mother for the cottage. You would also go to school and learn skills—I dare say you'd get on first-rate with all your experience in needlework. What do you say?"

"Oh, sir, it sounds lovely, it does. I weren't never one for charity, but I would give 'most anything for some food right now. An' Emmy's hungry, too. I don't think I would ha' gone before, but I don't much like the penny lodging-house, an' I don't even have the penny. Would they take us, sir? I could try to clean Emmy up a bit—she ain't had a bath in ever so long."

"They will take you both just as you are. We'll have some food first. There's a bakery in the next street, isn't there? I thought so. Now, what will we do with your stool? You won't need it where you're going."

"If you please, sir, there's the Baineses in the next house. There's lots of 'em and hardly any chairs. They could have it if they like."

"Run in quickly and give it to them, and then we'll be off."

Katie put Emmy down, disappeared into the house and emerged with a smile a few moments later. "All right, sir. They was very thankful."

Mr. Warren bent down and picked up Emmy, and the three of them made their way down the road, past the costers, the drunk men, the boys playing at pitch and toss; away from the quarrelling women, the begging dogs, the children playing in the gutter; away from Nichols Street: away from hunger, ignorance, and poverty.

Chapter 10

As spring gave way to summer, Jack was released from the infirmary and was given the bed next to Ned's. Jack was also put into the bakery, and for hours every afternoon the two boys helped there. Since they were the newest and youngest boys in the bakery, they had all the odd jobs: making sure the ovens had plenty of coal, bringing drinks of water to those working near the ovens, fetching more buckets of coal from the coal bin, and transferring the baked loaves from the cooling racks to trays.

At school, both boys progressed rapidly. Ned, especially, became a good reader, and by autumn could read most of the books in the Home's "library." This was composed of two tall bookcases in the schoolroom, filled with books which had been contributed by various friends and patrons of the institution. Some of the books were rather old, as so many donated things are, but the Home was thankful to have them, nonetheless. On a rainy November evening, Ned looked over the books and saw one titled *The Boys' Week-Day Book.* He took it from the shelf and turned the pages. There were illustrations, which interested him, and he could see little poems scattered throughout. One couplet caught his eye:

> Now look about you, little Ned
> And get some wisdom in your head.

That decided him. The charm of seeing his own name in print could not be resisted. He wrote the name of the book, his name, and the date in the little notebook which was kept near the shelves for that purpose, and took his find away to his dormitory. He sat on his bed and began to read.

> It should never be forgotten that 'As the twig is bent the tree's inclined.' We cannot reasonably hope that telling foolish stories will make any one wise, or that a bad boy will make a good man, and, therefore, if we wish the man to be upright, the boy must be well taught and properly corrected.

As the twig is bent the tree's inclined? What does that mean? wondered Ned. He read over the paragraph again. *Oh, I see,* he thought. *Whatever way you start growing is the way you keep growing.* He kept on reading.

> Whenever evil things draw nigh
> And sin along the pathway steals
> Then boys and girls should swiftly fly
> As though a bear were at their heels.

Where truth and meekness raise their head

Like flowerets on a mountain's crest

Climb up the steep with fearless tread,

And pluck and plant them in your breast.

Children often begin to practise deceit at an early age. A boy in petticoats once crouched down under a gooseberry-bush to pluck the fruit. 'What are you doing there?' cried his mother. 'O,' replied the youthful deceiver, 'I am only driving the flies away from the gooseberries!' Now the very same spirit which led this child to deceive his mother about the gooseberries, would, if not corrected, lead him in after life to deceive, to cheat his fellow men in things of greater value.

Just then Dick came into the dormitory and went to the box beneath his bed to get his little bag of marbles.

"Dick, what's gooseberries?" asked Ned.

"Ain't you had gooseberry pie?" said Dick.

"No," said Ned.

"Well, they're berries, ain't they—a kind o' fruit. Never mind about that now." He closed the lid of the box and walked back to the door. "Me an' Jack are playing marbles. You want to play?"

"All right," said Ned. He stood up slowly and stretched. Dick, who waited for no one, was out the door before he had finished his stretch. "Coming?" Dick called down the hall.

"Yes," answered Ned. His hand went to pick up the open book from the bed, but he was a little too quick or too careless. At any rate, his fingers grasped only a page or two instead of the covers. The book lifted off the bed for a moment before the pages ripped and the book fell back onto the bed. Pieces of the pages that had ripped were still in Ned's hand.

As a street Arab he had learned well what to do when something was damaged, and out of habit he looked hastily around to see if anyone had seen what happened. No, he was alone. He examined the book: two pages torn—half of each page ripped out. He thought for a moment. It was an old book, wasn't it? He turned to the title page and saw that it had been published in 1833—nearly fifty years before. Who would know when the damage was done? He could just quietly return the book to the schoolroom tomorrow, and with luck, no one would ever know. He set the book in the box under his bed, put the torn pages in his pocket, and went to play marbles.

Ned put the book back on the bookshelf the next morning without any feelings of remorse and surreptitiously fed the torn pages to the bakery oven without any pangs of guilt. He was only anxious to know that he would not be blamed and punished. A week went by, then two, and Ned forgot to think of the ripped pages in the book. And then one day, as the students were dismissed from the schoolroom, the master called to him to remain behind the others. Ned lingered near his seat as the other boys left, and the master waited until they were gone before coming to him with *The Boys' Week-Day Book* in his hand.

"John Kelly borrowed this book yesterday and found that two pages had been ripped out," said the Master. "You were the last to borrow the book, according to the record in the notebook. Do you know anything about it?"

Without so much as the blink of an eye, Ned said, "No, sir."

"The pages were ripped when you borrowed it, were they?"

"Yes, sir," said Ned.

"Very well," said the Master. "You are dismissed."

Ned went down to his dinner feeling vaguely discontent. He was not really a hardened liar. Other boys who continually got into scrapes and lied their way out of them were much more practiced in the art than he. He had told lies before, but never to people who were themselves perfectly honest. The Master was always truthful, and the deceit made Ned uncomfortable. *Well*, he told himself, *I got away with it; that is the great thing.* But as the day went on he could not quite get rid of the uneasy feeling.

As it happened, the next day's copywork contained a quotation from Alexander Pope: "Just as the twig is bent, the tree's inclined." Ned remembered the sentence, and as he copied it out several times, making sure that each letter was formed correctly, he remembered also the story about the little boy who lied about the gooseberries. *As the twig is bent, the tree's inclined.* A little boy who would tell lies about gooseberries might become a man who would lie about important things. He remembered a man from Button-hole Row, Jim, who was the biggest liar in the district. No one could believe anything he said. *As the twig is bent, the tree's inclined.* A boy who would lie about damaging a book might become a man who would lie about where he got his money. *As the twig is bent, the tree's inclined.* Mr. Langley and Mr. Warren must have been good boys, because they were good men. He would rather be like them than Jim. But his twig was bending in the wrong direction.

Ned had less appetite for lunch that day than he had ever had. He passed the rest of the day in a kind of fog; he did his laundry, worked in the bakery, played football, and went through all the other activities of the day in a very distracted frame of mind. That night he got his nightclothes on and sat on his bed, like all the other boys, to hear Mr. Langley conduct evening prayers. It was Mr. Langley's habit to read a little bit of Scripture each night before praying. He was reading the parables of Jesus, as the little stories seemed to catch the attention of the boys much better than some of the longer didactic passages. This evening he turned to the Gospel of Matthew, chapter thirteen, and read the parable of the wheat and the tares. When he had finished reading the parable, he skipped the next few verses and read Jesus' explanation of it.

> The Son of man shall send forth His angels, and they shall gather out of His kingdom all things that offend, and them which do iniquity; and shall cast them into a furnace of fire: there shall be wailing and gnashing of teeth. Then shall the righteous shine forth as the sun in the kingdom of their Father. Who hath ears to hear, let him hear.

Mr. Langley closed the Bible and prayed a simple prayer, asking God to watch over the boys in the night and to turn all of them that were tares into good wheat. He bid the boys goodnight, turned out the light, and walked back to his little room down the hall. He got ready for bed himself, and as was his habit, prayed for each of the boys in his dormitory by name. Then he got into his bed and turned out the lamp.

The next morning Mr. Langley got up, read his Bible, and went about his duties. He woke the boys, supervised their washing and dressing, inspected their made beds, and made sure they were all assembled in the dining room on time for morning prayers and breakfast. After breakfast, he took one of the boys to the Resident

Master; the boy had been openly rebellious to Mr. Langley and needed discipline. Only the Governor of the Home and the Resident Master were allowed to punish the boys, and Mr. Langley was sure that judgement would be firm but not cruel. In the afternoon he prepared reports on the number of infractions of rules by the boys and how they had been dealt with. Dr. Barnardo liked to have reports on everything, which was good, but it was hard for those who had to spend so much time on them.

After supper, during free time, it was his custom to read in his room with the door open. The boys knew they could come in and talk to him, and often a lad with something on his mind took advantage of that quiet hour to unburden himself. He was just settling down to read *The Memoirs of McCheyne* when Ned appeared at the door, looking extremely troubled.

"Yes, Ned? Have you something to tell me?" Ned nodded. "Come in and shut the door, if you like. Now then, what is it you'd like to say?"

"Sir, I told a lie." The words burst forth from Ned with no preamble. The parable Mr. Langley had read the night before had dominated his thoughts since he heard it, causing a nearly-sleepless night and feelings of misery and guilt until he was desperate. "I told a lie, and that's wicked, ain't it?"

Mr. Langley was surprised at the abrupt confession from such a quiet boy, but he did not hesitate in answering. "Yes, telling a lie is very wicked. Satan, who is God's worst enemy, is called the father of lies."

"I'm wicked then," said Ned in a sort of calm despair. "An' last night you were reading about the wicked people being thrown in the fire."

"Yes." Mr. Langley pulled out his Bible and turned to the passage in Matthew. "Yes, it says, 'and they shall gather out of his kingdom all things that offend, and them which do iniquity; and shall cast them into a furnace of fire: there shall be wailing and gnashing of teeth.' Did that trouble you, Ned?"

"I was lookin' at the oven in the bakery today, and it was awful hot. I don't want to go into the fire, sir. But I told that lie, and now I have to go to Hell, don't I, sir?"

"You were wicked before you told that lie, Ned. Your telling the lie didn't make you wicked; you told the lie because you were already wicked, do you see?" Ned looked at him blankly. He tried again. "Do you think that if you hadn't told the lie, you wouldn't be in trouble with God?"

Ned nodded.

"That's where you're wrong. You've done lots of wicked things; in fact, you've been doing them all your life. You haven't felt guilty over them, but they were wrong just the same. You were in trouble with God long before you told the lie."

"It's all up with me, then. No hope."

"Every hope in the world, Ned. But first you must understand that we're all wicked, every one of us. Did you ever hear this verse? 'There is none righteous, no not one: there is none that understandeth, there is none that seeketh after God.' That makes every person on the earth a wicked person. And God has the right to send us all to Hell. But instead of doing that, He did something else. Do you know what that was?"

Ned shook his head.

"He sent Jesus into the world to die on the cross. You've heard that Jesus died on the cross, haven't you? Tell me, why did He die on the cross?"

"For our sins."

"Exactly. Jesus died to take care of all the sins of anyone who would believe on Him. And if we trust in Him, He will save us." Mr. Langley looked at the child before him and wondered how much he understood.

Ned thought for a moment, and then spoke. "If I believe in Him, He'll let me off goin' to Hell?"

"Yes, indeed."

"An' what'll I do to make up for the lie?"

"It's not like that, Ned. You could never make up for the lie—or indeed, any of the other wrong things you have done. No. Wickedness is too bad for us to be able to do anything about it ourselves. That is why Jesus had to die. But when you trust in Christ and God makes you his child, he gives you a pardon—He forgets every single wrong thing you have done, and gives you a new heart that doesn't want to do wicked things."

The light of understanding broke on Ned's face. All the Bible lessons and scripture verses that had been taught to him over the last year suddenly made sense.

"You go away and think about it," said Mr. Langley, "And we can talk again tomorrow if you would like to. Soon, perhaps, you will be ready to repent of your sins and become a child of God."

"Thank you, sir," said Ned. He opened the door and went out into the hallway, but before he had gone three steps he turned around and came back into the room.

"Sir, do I have to?"

"Do you have to do what?"

"Wait, sir. Do I have to wait 'til tomorrow to become a child of God? I don't want to wait."

"No, if you feel like that, you don't need to wait. We will pray then." Mr. Langley knelt with the boy on the floor and prayed a simple prayer, asking God to help Ned understand that he was a sinner, and needed a Saviour, and that Christ was his only hope. And then Ned prayed. It was not an eloquent prayer: he stumbled over the words and repeated himself a great deal. But it was the cause of great rejoicing in heaven.

Chapter 11

1882

The warm June sun streamed through the windows of Mr. Appleton's office as Mr. Fielder, the governor of the Stepney Home, sat talking with the Resident Master.

"I have spoken with Dr. Barnardo this morning," said Mr. Fielder. "You know that we have been sending a few boys every year to Canada and other countries with different children's emigration societies. It has helped to provide room in the Home for more boys, and it has helped to fill the great need for workers in Canada. The boys who have gone seem to be doing well. The Doctor now feels it is time to set up our own emigration scheme. We will provide an outfit and passage for a group of boys every year to go to Canada. He has an agent there, a Mr. Owen, who will distribute them to farms in need of workers. Now, we need to choose fifty boys to be the pioneers, as it were, of this new venture. They will sail in August."

"August! And this is already June! Well, we have our work before us, then. Fifty boys, you say? How will we choose the fifty?"

"The Doctor believes that it would be best to send older boys, between the ages of fourteen and seventeen. He wants the best we have; "the flower of the flock" was the phrase he used. Good-tempered, hard-working, and strong lads—they are the ones who will be useful there, you know, and give emigration a good name. There are those in Canada who see the emigration of children as the dumping of unwanted little criminals into their fresh, new country."

"I understand. Well, I will look over the records and see which boys are the correct ages and we will narrow the list down from there."

"Thank you. I will need to go to Liverpool and make arrangements for their passage, as well as purchasing trunks and clothing for them. I will come and see you next week and we can go over the list together then."

That afternoon, Ned and Jack went to the bakery as usual. They had been at the Home for over a year and they had been promoted from being coal-and-water fetchers to actually helping to make bread. They were still not strong enough to do the kneading, and the Master Baker preferred an older boy to mix the ingredients for the dough, but they were able to punch down the dough when it was required and to shape the dough into muffins, rolls, or loaves.

When Ned arrived in the bakery, his first task (after washing his hands) was to get one of the bowls of dough that had been set on a table near the oven to rise by the Master Baker. He brought the bowl over to one of the working tables, took off the cloth covering it, and quickly plunged his fist into the puffy dough. Immediately the dough sank down and Ned took it out of the bowl and put it on the table which had been sprinkled with flour. Then he made balls of dough and set them on a tray with some space between them. It did not take all of his attention to do this, and while he worked, he watched John kneading some dough next to him. John took the lump of dough and pushed it down with his hand until it was slightly flattened. Then he folded the dough over and pushed it down again. Then he folded it the other way and flattened it and kept working the dough in this way for several minutes until the dough was pliable and no longer sticky. Ned liked John; he was a strong lad, about age fifteen, and he was kind to the younger boys. Once, he had let Ned try to knead the dough, and Ned was surprised at how much effort it took to flatten the dough and fold it over. John's strong hands could do it so quickly that it looked easy.

Ned finished making his tray of rolls, covered it with a cloth and put it back on the rack near the oven to rise again. He had just got another bowl of dough when the Master Baker brought a new boy over to the table where they were working.

"This is Frank Sellon," said the Master. Ned and Jack looked at each other, and Jack nodded slightly. It was the Basher they had known at the Ragged School. It had been over a year since they had seen him, but he still had that arrogant look and swaggering walk.

"Jack, you show Frank what he is to do." And the Master turned to Peter, who had been doing the odd jobs, and began to instruct him in the art of sifting flour, which would be one of his new tasks.

Jack sighed. Frank had lived in Bethnal Green, and Jack had known him even before that day at the Ragged School. The sly grin on Frank's face told him that he remembered him, too.

"Come on," said Jack, and Frank followed him out to where the coal was kept. "'Ere's the coal bin," said Jack. "When they tells you the oven needs more coal, you get this bucket here an' fill it with coal an' bring it in. And I'll show you the water." He led him back inside to a large wooden bucket sitting on a table in the corner. "The ones as are working near the ovens gets over-hot sometimes, and they need a drink o' water. Yer job is to make sure it don't get empty and take 'em a drink when they're too busy to get it themselves. There's a tap near the coal bin where you can fill it. An' the cooling racks are over here. When these are cool—*these* ones ain't cool enough yet—you take 'em off the rack and put 'em in baskets. Loaves in these, rolls in those, and muffins in that. Lemme see...these rolls are cool enough. Feel 'em. When they feel like that, you can put 'em in baskets."

Frank rolled his eyes. "It ain't much of a job," he complained. "A baby could do that. I want to put things in and out of the ovens."

"*You* don't decide what yer going to do," said Jack. "The master does that. All new boys do these jobs first. You put them rolls in that basket. I have to go back to my work."

Frank put the rolls in the basket. When that was done, there was coal to be fetched and then water, and then more bread was cooled enough to be put into baskets. On the streets, there had always been boys who would join him in mischief, ready to defy authority along with him, and he had been trying all morning to get someone else in trouble with him. But in this room everyone was too industrious to pay attention to him. He kept busy for an hour doing his various tasks, and once when he stopped working and just stood watching the kneaders, he was told sharply to get back to his job.

"More coal!" came a call, and Frank went to fetch some. He put two lumps of coal into his pocket before coming into the bakery again, and continued going about his duties until he saw an opportunity. John had left off his kneading for a moment to get a drink of water, and Ned, who was working next to John, was particularly absorbed in his work. Frank pulled one lump of coal from his pocket and dexterously poked it into the ball of dough that John had left. The other lump of coal he let fall on the floor next to Ned's feet, covering the sound with a loud cough. He then retreated to the far end of the bakery to check the bread on the cooling racks.

In less than a moment, John was back at his kneading, and it was only a few seconds before the lump of coal was discovered in the dough, discolouring and ruining it.

The master baker was called and shown the damage. Frank watched the master's eyes slide over Ned and the other boys and focus on himself.

"Frank!" the master beckoned sternly. Frank sauntered over.

"Why did you put the lump of coal in the dough?"

"It weren't me, sir, honest! It must ha' been someone else." He dropped his gaze to the floor in what he hoped looked like an expression of innocent humility. He gave an exaggerated start and a little gasp of surprise. "Oh, look here, sir! It's like to ha' been this boy here" (pointing to Ned) "who had another piece o' coal and dropped it accidental."

He looked up to see how the master took this accusation, but the master did not so much as glance at Ned. He had been in charge of the bakery at the Barnardo home for five years, and this was by no means the first wily boy to try to set a trap for another.

"John, you're Frank's minder," he said to that youth, and then returned to his work.

"All right then, Frank," said John with a sigh. "Put the coal back where it belongs."

"But it weren't—" began Frank.

"No use," said John. "Better not try."

Frank opened his mouth, looked at John's face and then at his strong arms, and closed his mouth. Reluctantly he took the coal that John was holding out to him and bent down and picked up the one on the floor, too. He was surprised to see John following him outside to see that the coal was returned to its bin.

"I don't need a shadow," said Frank sullenly.

"You do," said John. "That's what a minder is. Bread's too important for you to be playing tricks with it. The master can't trust you, so he's given you a shadow for a time."

Frank rolled his eyes.

"It's a bother for me," said John, "because I can't do near so much work when I have to shadow you. And it's a bother for you, because all the time you're not fetching coal or water or putting the bread on trays, you'll have to stand next to me. But the sooner you get trustworthy, the sooner you won't need a minder. Now, it ain't worth it for you to get sulky like that. You'll only need a minder longer. Get back inside now—they'll be needing those cooling racks cleared."

In spite of John's admonitions, Frank finished his time in the bakery in a decidedly resentful spirit. Like other bullies, Frank was apt to take the just consequences of his actions as a grievance. The worst of it was that he was left to pity himself, as no one else had leisure or inclination to show sympathy for his petulance. On the streets he was feared, and he gloried in the grudging respect paid by other street boys. But here...

He went outside with the other boys for physical exercises and games, and relieved his feelings by pushing a little boy when he thought no one was looking. The Games Master, however, had seen him, and he was punished by having to sit on a bench during the whole of the game.

That evening found Jack, Ned, and Dick playing their usual game of marbles.

"That new chap Frank's a bit of a tough, ain't he?" said Dick.

"Always was," said Jack.

"Maybe he'll run away," suggested Ned. Some of the most difficult boys had in times past taken themselves off, to the relief of the rest of the Home and the peril of the larger population of London.

"I'll pray he runs away," said Jack.

"But *that* won't do 'im much good," said Dick.

"Do *him* good?" repeated Ned. He had been pleased that day to see Frank in trouble for his misdeeds and felt that he had got a kind of revenge on him. As for doing Frank good...his thoughts had never wandered in that direction.

"Why not?" asked Dick. "Ain't we supposed to want everybody's good?"

"Well, but *Frank*..." said Jack.

"Yes," said Dick, "that's the point. Frank. You oughter listen better when Mr. Langley reads to us afore bed. Your go," he said to Jack, and the game progressed without any further reference to Frank.

That night as Ned lay in bed waiting for sleep to come, he remembered what Dick had said. What had he meant about listening to Mr. Langley? His mind reviewed the last few nights' Bible readings. Mr. Langley was reading through Christ's long sermon in the Gospel of Matthew, and Ned had been at the Home long enough to have become familiar with the passage. Three nights ago had been the bit about swearing vows, two nights ago had been about turning the other cheek—was that was Dick had meant? Last night... what was last night? Oh, yes; last night had been the part about loving your enemies—ah! That was what he had meant. There had been something about praying for enemies, too, hadn't there?

A rebellious impulse hardened his heart for a moment. He didn't want to pray for his enemy, except perhaps to pray that he would go away! He called to mind the scene over a year ago when Frank had tricked the coster into hitting him. Bitterness twisted something inside him. But the words of Scripture have a funny way of sticking to you, forcing themselves into your mind and giving you no peace until you obey them. *"Love your enemies... pray for them..."* Ned tossed on his bed and tried to think of other things, but it was no good. His conscience would not let him rest.

All right, he thought at last, giving up the struggle. *I suppose I must. O God, help Frank to...erm...stop being bad, and to be...well...a good boy...and to listen to the Bible readings...and to...to honour the Queen. Amen. There, I've done it.* And his conscience, appeased, allowed him to sleep.

Chapter 12

Subdued excitement was the tenor of the Home in the following weeks as fifty boys prepared to leave and make their home in Canada. To the chagrin of the younger residents, all their favourite older boys were chosen to go, John from the bakery among them. The "pioneer" boys had a special meeting to teach them what to expect in Canada, and were given warm coats and caps with ear flaps in anticipation of cold winters. In the middle of August they left for their new country and morning prayers for two weeks included a petition for the travellers. A loud cheer went up when it was announced that the party had arrived safely in Canada.

Ned doggedly prayed for Frank without much apparent fruit, although Frank had ceased much of his bullying as the masters became acquainted with his tendencies and kept a determined eye on him. After being caught and punished in numerous attempts to cause trouble, he became tolerably well-behaved, although his attitude remained sullen and he appeared to view everything he didn't like as a personal affront.

The following spring, a hundred boys followed the first fifty, and the atmosphere of the Home changed. Of course boys had been coming to and leaving the Home constantly since Ned had arrived, but never *en masse*. The empty places filled rapidly with new boys who needed to be trained in the ways of the Home, and the knowledge that many of the boys now resident would likely go to Canada before long meant that an air of expectancy pervaded the place. Ned rather disliked the change. Having been so long unsettled, he had valued the sense of permanency in the Home; he had never been afraid that he would be forced out to make his own way again, and that had been a comfort. Now there seemed to be a feeling of transience.

On a warm June morning, it was the turn of Ned's dormitory to miss school in order to help prepare the midday meal in a stifling kitchen. Dick was thrilled, as usual, to be let off school, but Ned would rather have been able to attend. The two boys stood side by side at one of the worktables, chopping a large pile of carrots.

"Got a letter from my sister at the Girls Village yesterday," Dick confided to Ned. "It's a queer thing, but she says she's goin' ter Canada!"

"By herself?" asked Ned.

"No, no. There's nigh on seventy of 'em going in August. Wish I could go with her."

"You? Go to Canada?" Ned's voice was troubled.

"Why not? D'you mean to say you don't want to go?"

"No, I don't."

"Whyever not? Canada's the best place for gettin' on. Work a few years for a farmer, save up a tidy bit, buy yer own farm, and there you have it!"

"I'd rather study than work on a farm," said Ned. "An' I like it here."

"Yer daft, you are. You can't go to school forever. What'll you do when you leave the Home? You'll work in a bakery or summat. I'd rather work on a farm than a bakery. Coo! There might be horses an' all. I'd like horses."

"Just the same, I want to stay here," said Ned. The spectre of leaving or having his friends leave chilled his heart in spite of the heat of the kitchen. He comforted himself with the knowledge that boys were not sent out until they were fourteen, and that though Dick would be fourteen next year, Ned and Jack would be secure for at least three more years.

*   *   *

"The boys were all placed out quickly, were they?" said Mr. Appleton to Mr. Fielder. The two men were back in Mr. Appleton's office almost exactly a year after their previous conference in the same place. Mr. Fielder had accompanied the group of a hundred boys to Canada, had seen them put into homes, and had now returned.

"Yes, very quickly. In two weeks they were all spoken for and gone. The land is crying out for labourers, Appleton. It's a grand opportunity for the boys. I hope the girls will be just as successful."

"I suppose I must get another list ready, then?"

"Yes, and this time we will be including younger boys in the party. Dr. Barnardo says that boys as young as six will be allowed to go—there are families willing to adopt them and bring them up as their own."

"Six, eh? That's very young."

"So it is, but it might be better for the children to get used to Canada as young as possible. It's a vastly different land, Appleton. The farms are more isolated than they are in England. Trees everywhere, rivers, lakes...I saw moose! Cold, though, in the winter. It was cool enough while we were there, and that was springtime. Younger children are more adaptable, you know."

"Yes, I see the advantages." Mr. Appleton paused a moment in thought. "I wonder, though... what if the farmers simply use the children for labour without really treating them like family members? I know there is a scheme set up for visitors to call on the families yearly and see that they are being well cared for, but once a year is not very often. You remember Doyle's report ten years ago—the cruelty that some emigrant children were exposed to. It's bad enough for the older boys, but I truly shudder to think of the younger ones being used in that way."

"I know." The enthusiasm in Mr. Fielder's face had dimmed. He got up from his chair and paced slowly around the room as he resumed talking. "And yet... And yet you know where most of these children come from. The ones who lived on the streets, the ones who lived half-starved with depraved and degraded parents...remember the boy who came with both arms broken because his father had beaten him? And there are thousands still in those circumstances. Scarcely anything could be worse than where they are. If they trade one kind of misery for another in spite of our precautions, then it will be very bad; but I cannot help but think that though the new misery would be dreadful, still, it would not last forever. There are opportunities in Canada that are unknown here. It seems well worth the risk..."

"And, as you say," said Mr. Appleton, "There *are* safeguards in place—we will be doing more than has ever been done before for child emigrants to ensure their safety and well-being."

"Yes, that is the view we must take. And the experience of travel is an advantage for the children, too. Byron's lines, 'Roll on, thou deep and dark blue ocean—roll!' will never be appreciated so well as they are by those who have actually sailed across the sea. Well, I should be going, Appleton. There's no great hurry about the list. I believe that we will be sending out a party of girls every Autumn and a party of boys every Spring. The list of boys need not be finalized until January."

*   *   *

January 12, 1884. The day dawned clear as glass and cold as granite. The boys were up before daybreak, of course, washing and dressing as quickly as they could. As they were making their beds, one of the masters nailed up two pieces of paper in the hallway between the dormitories. It was the Canada List. As soon as the first boy discovered what it was, the hall was filled with boys, jostling, squirming and straining to see which names were on it. Finally, those nearest the list began reading out the names. They were listed in alphabetical order, and Ned waited through the first few letters of the alphabet with a beating heart.

"Fredrick Dodson... Michael Doherty... Oliver Drayman... John Ellis... George Epworth... Jack Ferris..."

Jack! Jack going to Canada? Ned's heart sank. To lose Jack! Names were still being read out.

"John Garry...Thomas Glinder... James Grant... Edward Harrison... Walter Henry... Warren Holmes..."

It took several moments for Ned to realize that *he* was Edward Harrison.

He was going to Canada.

Chapter 13

Liverpool, England, 1884

One hundred boys stood in rows, shivering in the early evening mist on a Liverpool dock and waiting for the signal to board the *S.S. Parisian*. Most of the boys wore wide grins and talked quietly among themselves about the ships surrounding them and exulting in the fact that their own ship appeared to be one of the largest. Ned had the feeling that he was the only one of the crowd who was not exhilarated by the smell of salt air and the cries of sea birds.

The shock and misery he had felt when he first learned that he was to go to Canada had lessened a bit during the following weeks. He had realized that even if he stayed in England, all his friends would be gone and that life in the Home would not be the same. Mr. Langley had been chosen to be one of Barnardo's staff who would escort the boys across the ocean, and as *he* was enthusiastic about the golden opportunity for all his boys, and as the other lads could hardly contain their excitement, Ned allowed himself to be swept along in the bustle without a murmur. He was eleven now, and no one should say that he was a baby to be crying after the old familiar things.

After three months of preparation, the day of departure dawned. The boys, dressed in their dark blue uniforms, had marched through the streets of London to Euston Station that morning, accompanied by Dr. Barnardo himself and the Home's band playing "Rescue the Perishing." There they had boarded a special train which had taken them to Liverpool. Most of them had never been out of London or on a train, and instead of the high spirits one might have expected from one hundred boys setting off on high adventure, there was rather a sense of wonder and a bit of apprehension—the unknown being so *very* unknown. They were mostly quiet, looking out the windows on pastureland, small towns, farms, and rivers.

Ned was seated near Dick and Jack, and the three of them talked quietly of the farm life they expected to have. That is to say, Dick and Jack talked, and Ned listened. Two hours into the train journey, Dr. Barnardo came through the carriages. He was a short man with spectacles and a walking stick, and his appearance was such that boys might be tempted to make sport of him. Somehow, though, they never did. He had an air of authority about him that put boys immediately in their place without him ever needing to raise his voice or use force. He spoke pleasantly to several of the boys, asking them questions about their ambitions and giving an encouraging word to some of the younger ones. One little boy named Bobby was only six, and was under the special care of Mr. Langley. The Doctor patted Bobby on the back and asked him if he would like to have a mother and father. Bobby nodded.

"You will have them, and shortly," said the Doctor. "And I will make it my prayer that you have the best parents that the Dominion can bestow."

After a journey of four hours, they arrived at Lime Street Station in Liverpool. There was another walk through the streets as the boys, carrying their travelling bags, made their way to the docks. The procession was followed by carts which carried the boys' one hundred trunks. The first sight of the docks brought gasps from most of the boys. An array of ships, many of them large steamers, were docked in the harbour. Some of the boys had seen boats on the Thames, but a large, ocean-going steamer was completely outside their experience.

Ned found himself walking next to little Bobby and Mr. Langley as they proceeded along the docks. It gave him a little bit of comfort that Mr. Langley would be with him during the journey.

"That's our ship there," said Mr. Langley, pointing to a large ship. It had three empty masts for sails, should they be needed, and a large funnel which was bright red with a black top and a white band around it. Flying from one of the masts was a red, white and blue flag under a long red pennant.

"That's the flag of the Allan Line, and the *Parisian* is an Allan ship," he explained.

The boys were brought to a halt on the wharf and were put into orderly rows while officials checked the destination and landing cards and made sure each boy was on the list of passengers. A short farewell speech and prayer came from the Doctor, and then each boy picked up his travelling bag and filed on board the ship.

"Steerage" was made up of several large rooms in the depths of the ship with hundreds of bunkbeds in each room. All told, there were a thousand beds on the steerage deck of the "Parisian," and several hundred more beds in the first and second class cabins above. The Barnardo boys were the first on board, having been given a special dispensation to get settled before the other travellers embarked the next day.

The boys were herded toward one section of steerage and told to choose a bed. Ned chose a top bunk, and was rather distressed to find that Frank took the bunk underneath his. Frank's behaviour in the Home had been acceptable enough that he had been allowed to go to Canada, but Ned was not convinced that he was a reformed character. Jack and Dick had their beds several rows away.

The boys were then taken to the mess hall: a large room with wooden tables and benches painted white. Stewards in white coats served a meal of steamed bacon and cabbage. They were introduced to Miss Coulson, the nurse who would be travelling with them, and Mr. Owen, who had come from Canada to help escort them across.

"He talks funny, don't 'e?" whispered Jack, after Mr. Owen had given a few words of greeting to the assembly.

"That's the way they talk in Canada," said Ned. "They say the words a bit different."

When they had eaten, the boys went back to their bunks and got ready for bed. The travel bags they had been given were not large, but besides night clothes each bag contained a new Sankey Hymn Book, a Bible, a *Traveller's Guide*, and *Pilgrim's Progress*. There was no time for reading them that night, however. After getting into bed, Mr. Langley read his usual passage of Scripture and prayed—at least that was one thing that was the same—and then the lamps were put out. How soon the other boys went to sleep Ned could not tell, for it was completely dark. He lay awake for many hours, though, wondering what the voyage would be like, and more importantly, what would be waiting for him at the end of it. *"Since the Lord Himself is there, 'tis not meet that we should fear,"* he reminded himself.

The next day was filled with waiting. The boys got out of their beds at the six o'clock call and queued up for their turn in the "wash house." After that there was the wait on deck for the signal to go down to breakfast. And after that there was a long, long wait for the other passengers to board the ship. Ned and Jack stood together with some other boys, looking over the railings of the ship at the people struggling up the gangway. A babble of languages fell on his ear, but of course he did not know what they were. The nurse, Miss Coulson, stood beside the boys, watching, too.

"Where are all those people from?" asked Jack.

"I asked one of the stewards that myself," said Miss Coulson. "He said they were German, Norwegian, English, Scotch, Irish and a few other nationalities. More Irish will join us when the ship stops in Londonderry tomorrow."

"Why are they all going to Canada?" asked Ned.

"A few of them are going for a visit, but most of them are emigrating, just as you are."

Ned looked at the people again. There were some young men who seemed to be travelling on their own or with friends, but there were also many families with children. Miss Coulson gave a little sigh and then spoke again, almost to herself.

"There are more opportunities for them in Canada than there are in their home countries. They will probably do very well, and their children will be grateful that the move was made, but..." she paused and looked down at a family with two young children struggling to carry their bags. "They are leaving everything behind. Their lives will never be the same again. Nothing will be the same for them."

Jack looked at the woman's pensive face. "Are *you* emigrating, too, miss?"

Miss Coulson shook her head. "No. At least...not yet." She smiled at them and left the railing.

The boys began to play a game, trying to guess whether each traveller would be in first class, second class, or steerage. The poorly dressed ones were easy to identify as steerage passengers, but the better dressed ones were more difficult.

The sun had begun to lower in the sky by the time that the last of the passengers had boarded the ship. A group of people on the docks cheered and waved as the anchor was raised and the ship moved away from the wharf. Ned saw some of the women wiping away tears. The boys were allowed to stay on deck as they watched the boat slide past the other ships and out into the Irish Sea. The slightly rolling motion of the ship became much more pronounced and the waves much bigger as they went further and further away from land. Before the coast of England had entirely disappeared, the Isle of Man came into view, and soon after that, the sun set and they could see no more.

They went below deck then, for the evening meal, and one after another began to feel a little sick. The up-and-down motion of the ship had been tolerable when they were up on deck, but being inside a closed room began to have its effect on their stomachs. Many of them only ate a little bit, and some who had a full meal soon regretted it. The stewards were kept busy for quite a long time, cleaning up after those who had lost their dinners. Some who had been feeling tolerably well felt much worse when presented with the sights and smells of their comrades vomiting around them.

When bedtime came, it was almost impossible for Ned to sleep. Aside from the seasickness, he was continually rolled from one side of his bed to the other. He did not know how he could possibly endure nine days of life on this ship. Eventually he fell asleep and dreamed that he was riding in a very bumpy carriage.

The next morning, the boys woke to find themselves in calm water again, docked in Londonderry Port. Another stream of emigrants boarded the ship, nearly all of them obviously steerage passengers. They were in high spirits, chattering to each other in Gaelic and sometimes in English, and choosing bunks together.

The steerage compartments were much more crowded now, though they were not full. Mr. Langley, when asked, gave his opinion that seven hundred of the thousand beds in steerage were occupied. The Barnardo boys and their escorts (except for the nurse) slept in one section, the single men in another section, the single women in another section, and the families in yet another place. And within those groups it seemed that the different nationalities were clustered together, so that it was very like little countries within the world of the ship.

When all the Irish passengers were on board, the ship glided out of the harbour and into the dark waters of the Atlantic Ocean. They would not see land again for over a week.

Chapter 14

T hey were four days out to sea when Mr. Langley brought Bobby to the nurse. The motion of the ship had unbalanced him as he was climbing the stairs and he had tumbled down a few steps, scraping his elbow rather badly and banging his head on the railing. Nurse Coulson was kind but brisk, and Bobby was all the braver for being treated like a man. Mr. Langley stayed with the boy while the lump on the head was examined and the wound cleaned and bandaged, and reminded him to thank the nurse when she was finished. They were just leaving when the whistle for the midday meal sounded.

"Will you be coming down to eat, Miss Coulson?" asked Mr. Langley.

"I will, as soon as I get these things put away."

"Well, Bobby," said Mr. Langley, "you'd better not be late. Go with Ned, here"—for Ned was just passing—"He'll take you down to the mess room. Thank you, Ned."

He turned back to the nurse, who was rolling up the leftover bandage. "Are you still suffering much from seasickness? I heard you felt quite ill the first few days out."

"I am some better, thank you," said Miss Coulson, smiling.

"You have done well to keep tending to the sick boys when you didn't feel well yourself."

"Ah, well, I knew that the seasick boys were routed out of bed no matter how they felt, made to wash and dress, go on deck, stand to attention, march down two flights of steps, sing grace and try to eat. I felt that in the face of such heroics, I simply could not pamper myself and stay in bed. I had hoped that the seasickness would be gone completely by now—most people seem to recover their appetites in that time—but the sea seems rougher today and I'm not feeling as lively as I was yesterday."

"Yes, I was on deck a little while ago; there was a strong wind and I saw some very dark clouds approaching. I would not be surprised if we were in for a good storm."

Miss Coulson's face sobered at once. "I was a little afraid of that," she said. "I do so hate the idea of a storm at sea."

"But there is little danger, you know," said Mr. Langley. "Steamships are built so well, and we are not near a coastline—no rocks to founder on—and there is no fog that might veil an approaching ship."

"I know. But heavy seas *can* cause a breach in the hull, even on a steamship."

"You seem to know more about it than most people."

Miss Coulson sighed. "I suppose I do. My family has a long acquaintance with the sea. Both my great-grandfather and my grandfather were ship's captains, and my father and uncle had ambitions in that direction as well. Father was a first officer and my uncle was second officer on the crew of the *Royal Charter*. He was lost in that wreck."

"I see," said Mr. Langley, his face now as grave as her own. The tragedy of the *Royal Charter* had happened twenty-five years before, but the disaster was such that most people knew about it.

"My father never recovered from his brother's death," said Miss Coulson. "He gave up his ambition to be a captain and became an engineer instead. He grew morose and bitter, always rehearsing the catastrophe of the lives lost so close to the shore—within a stone's throw! I suppose I have caught a little of his gloomy view," she finished, trying to smile and not succeeding very well.

"I can well understand your fears," said Mr. Langley sympathetically. "I have always felt that it is entirely possible to know too much about possible dangers, although *you* cannot help your knowledge."

"No, I cannot." She finished putting away the last of the medicines and bandages that had been used in the course of the morning and looked for a moment out of the little round window of her cabin. She turned back to Mr. Langley with more confidence in her face.

"However, I have not forgotten Who controls the wind and the waves. I'm sure I should be paralyzed with fear if I could not trust His wisdom and power. And He is so good to remind me of it. Only yesterday, I passed a boy in the passageway and he was humming to himself—the tune was the hymn 'When We Cannot See Our Way.' Do you know, I have not sung that hymn in years, but the words came back then...you know the lines: 'Though the sea be deep and wide...Fearless let us still proceed, since the Lord vouchsafes to lead.'

The words seemed very appropriate for a traveller by sea! And then this morning, when I woke and the sea seemed rougher, other words of the hymn came back to me, like 'Since the Lord Himself is there, 'tis not meet that we should fear.' I was very much comforted."

"Hymns can be very sustaining," agreed Mr. Langley. "During a dangerous illness, I was helped by Baxter's hymn that says, 'Christ leads me through no darker rooms than He went through before.' And my father—but if I tell you that story we will certainly miss the meal that is even now being served." He offered her his arm as he said, "Shall we go down to see if the food on the tables can tempt your appetite at all?"

"Yes, thank you. I may as well 'give it a go,' as the boys say," she replied, smiling as she took his arm.

Ned had not been enjoying himself much on the journey. The boys were taken on deck to do exercises several times a day, and it frightened him a little to look over the ship's railings and see nothing but water all around. The ship which had seemed so large docked in Liverpool shrank into insignificance compared with the immense, dark, rolling ocean, and the sky that came all the way down to meet the sea. As long as he could remember, Ned had been surrounded by the buildings of London, which reduced the sky to a square patch overhead. Now he could see that the sky was as vast as the ocean. They were completely alone in their little ship that bobbed about on the water. If they sank, there would be no one to help them. He tried not to look over the side of the ship very often.

Down below deck there were other problems. The air was close and stale. He was much more queasy when there was no horizon to look at and there was not much to do. Marbles were not possible when the floor was constantly moving, and reading made him feel even worse. He spent some of his time in conversation with the other boys, and made friends with little Bobby. Bobby had, in his turn, made friends with one of the other little boys in steerage—one of the Irish children. Though they did not speak the same language, Bobby and Liam still managed to play together, crawling under the bunkbeds and hiding when adults passed by. Liam's mother smiled at Bobby whenever she saw him, and said, "Buachaill maith[12]," which meant nothing at all to Bobby. When the Irish passengers sat together and sang songs like "Mo Ghile Mear," Bobby hummed along and tried to say the foreign words.

Ned now took Bobby down to the steerage dining room and helped him cut his food. The sea was definitely rougher than it had been: the water in the glasses had a tendency to slosh onto the clothes of the boys when they tried to drink, and many who thought they had done with seasickness found that it was returning. Frank was one of these. For all Ned's fears at the beginning of the voyage, Frank had been a most docile bunk-mate. This was due, no doubt, to the fact that Frank had been very seasick for much of the journey and spent most of his free time in his bed, groaning at regular intervals. He had felt a little better this last day or so, however, and had managed to eat a good-sized breakfast and a moderate lunch. Now he was regretting it. Feeling distinctly uncomfortable, he asked Mr. Langley for permission to leave the mess room and go back to bed. He crawled back into his bunk and lay there panting and hoping the nausea would pass.

When lunch was finished, Mr. Langley thought that a vigorous march around deck would help some of the boys who were looking rather green, and so organized them into their customary columns and gave a brisk order to march up the stairs. Just as they started off, he

[12] Buachaill maith = pronounced something like "boohill my"; it means "good boy"

remembered Frank and wondered if some time on deck might help him as well. He sent Ned to see if Frank could be roused to join them. Ned was not feeling too well himself, and was torn between a desire to get some fresh air and a desire to stay well away from the sight of the dark, tempestuous sea. But Mr. Langley's orders must be obeyed, of course, and he hurried to the sleeping compartment.

"Frank!" he called, and heard a groan in reply. He made his way through the maze of bunkbeds until he was next to Frank's. "Mr. Langley wants you to come on deck with the rest of us—we're havin' a march 'round to clear our heads."

"I can't," whimpered Frank. "I can't. I'm goin' to be sick. Get me a basin or summat."

But before Ned could move to get one, it was too late. Frank seemed to go on being sick for a long, long, time. Ned did not know what to do. It seemed heartless to abandon Frank while he was still retching and gasping, so he stood there, trying his utmost not to be sick himself. Finally, Frank appeared to be done and lay weakly back in his bed, under the filthy, reeking blanket. Something would have to be done about that blanket.

"I'll find a steward," said Ned, and started back through the bunkbeds to the mess room. It seemed to him that the sea was even rougher than before; he stumbled several times and once his shoulder was knocked smartly on the iron bar of one of the bunkbeds. When he got to the mess room, it was empty and there were no stewards about—everyone seemed to have vanished. *Oh well,* he thought, *I must just do somethin' myself. Ugh. O God, please help me. I don't want to.*

He staggered back to Frank. "I can't find anyone," he said. "I'll try and do somethin'." He tugged gently at the bottom of the blanket until it came out from under the end of the mattress and then folded each side of the blanket inward, covering the mess and making a clumsy bundle out of it. As he did this, he heard a rumble of thunder, loud enough to distinguish above the sound of the engine, which they had by this time grown accustomed to. At the same time, the ship was definitely rocking more violently than it had—it was evident that this was a very bad storm.

"I daren't try to take yer blanket anywhere now," said Ned. "I'd fall, sure. But I can put it on the floor under the bed. There, now."

"Thanks," said Frank quietly, and then after a minute, "I wish I had a drink."

Ned shook his head. "I can't get any now. You'll have to wait."

Instead of complaining, as Ned rather expected him to, Frank nodded and closed his eyes.

"Maybe it won't be long 'til the storm's over," said Ned, though a violent rolling of the ship at that moment gave little hope of that. "I hope they all got off the deck," he added, almost to himself. "They'd be well overboard by this time."

He reached over to his own travelling bag and pulled out his handkerchief.

"Lemme wipe you off a bit. You're a sight, you are," he said, sitting down on the bed beside Frank.

Frank opened his eyes in surprise at this bit of friendliness. *He would never have done such service for another boy, especially one who had bullied him and his friends.*

"Thanks," he murmured again.

From the direction of the mess hall came the sound of boys' voices—a hundred of them—singing in unison:

"Eternal father strong to save;

Whose arm hath bound the restless wave,

Who bidst the mighty ocean deep

Its own appointed limits keep

Oh! hear us when we cry to Thee

For those in peril on the sea."

Evidently they had got off the deck all right.

Another peal of thunder came from overhead. Ned wondered what sound the ship would make if it broke apart. Would it sound like the thunder or would it be more like that house that fell down on Mead Street years ago? He looked at Frank. Frank's eyes were closed, as if he were sleeping, but a tear slid out from under his lashes and rolled down the side of his face. The ship lurched again, and a sound very like a sob came from Frank. He opened his eyes.

"D'you think we're goin' to sink?" he said.

"I dunno," said Ned.

"I don't want to die," said Frank with another sob. "If all them things is true—about Hell an' God an' sin an' all—then I don't want to die!" At this he began to cry in earnest, and Ned had no idea what to do. Gingerly he patted the older boy's shoulder, hoping it would give some comfort. But was comfort what Frank needed? It was fear that had brought Ned to Christ; perhaps fear would do the same for Frank. But what to say to him? Ned could think of nothing.

"I've been bad, ain't I?" said Frank. Ned could only nod. "An' there's no hope for me."

Ned seized on that. "Every hope in the world," he said, remembering Mr. Langley's words to himself all those months ago. "Jesus died for sinners, didn't 'e? An' that's what you are, an' that's what I am an' everyone else, too. Here, I'll read you a bit."

Ned reached back into his travelling bag and pulled out his Bible. His own nausea had lessened as he had helped Frank, and he prayed that reading would not make it return. He opened his Bible to the book of Romans and began reading at the third chapter. Frank continued to sob, and Ned nearly gave it up. But he decided to keep at it until Frank told him to stop. By the end of the chapter, Frank was listening quietly. At the end of chapter four, Frank was listening with his eyes closed. And when Ned looked up at the end of chapter five, Frank had fallen asleep. Ned closed the Bible, and noticed for the first time that the ship was not rolling as much as it had been. He put his Bible back into his bag and tottered his way to the mess room to join the other boys.

Chapter 15

Near Mount Forest, Ontario, Canada

M artha Johnson poured her husband another cup of coffee and cleared his empty porridge bowl and spoon from off the kitchen table. Her face was puckered a little with anxiety. Sam was tired; she could see it in the droop of his shoulders and in the lines around his eyes. *He ought not to work so hard*, she thought, but knew better than to say it aloud. There was nothing else to be done. The hired man had broken his leg badly, and had gone back to his sister's house to be nursed by her. And young Jimmy from down the road would have been able to come during the day and help, only his father had been laid up with rheumatism and could not spare the seventeen-year-old from his own farm.

"I've been thinking," said Sam, slowly stirring sugar into his coffee. "I must get some help."

Martha nodded and sat down at the table with him. She was still a young woman, though the extra burden of the last few weeks had taken away some of the freshness from her face. She had helped Sam all she could with the chores as well as doing the housework. "It's a blessing you've got no children, that's what," Mrs. MacDonald had said last week. "You'd not be able to do much outdoors if you had a baby." Martha had tried to think of it as a blessing that she had no children, but it was difficult. *I'd manage to help all the same,* she thought. *If I had a baby I'd be so thankful I could do anything. We'd manage...oh, we'd manage fine.*

Sam took a sip of his coffee and looked out the kitchen window. "There's no one I can think of that we can hire to help, and it's spring..."

Martha nodded again. Spring was almost as busy as harvest time: there was maple sap to be collected and made into syrup, the spring planting of vegetables and crops to be done, and of course, the daily chores which were constant no matter what the season. If only the hired man had broken his leg in the winter and been able to work again now!

"There was that notice in the newspaper," Sam went on, "about those boys coming out from England to work on farms. I was thinking..." he paused and looked at his wife. "We might get one of them."

It was Martha's turn to gaze out of the kitchen window at the little mounds of snow that were nearly finished melting on the muddy ground. She could see the hole in the barn roof that needed repairing— Jake, the hired man, had been on the ladder about to fix it, when Maisy, the obstreperous cow, had felt the urge to scratch her shoulder on the ladder, and down came Jake, breaking his leg. Jake knew everything about farming, and could have fixed that hole even better than Sam could.

"Would one of those English boys know anything about farming?" she asked.

"I wouldn't say they'd know much," said Sam. "The paper said that they teach the boys about Canadian life before they come, but I don't suppose they know how to plough. It did say that all the boys were chosen for their 'willingness to work hard and learn new things.' After all, it might not take too long to teach him most of the chores. And even if he knew nothing, to have a strong seventeen-year-old to help in repairing that fence or hauling logs or splitting firewood—that would make things much easier."

"Yes, that's so," agreed Martha. "Are they all that age?"

"Mostly, I think," said Sam. "You can request what age you want. I'd get a boy that's at least sixteen."

"See if you can find one that's been on a farm before," said Martha.

"I'll try, though I don't know if it's possible."

"How soon can we get one?"

"Soon. I hope we're not too late. The paper said the boys were arriving next week." He sneezed.

"I hope you're not getting ill," said his wife with concern. "Perhaps you'd better rest today."

"Not today, Martha. I'm behindhand with too much. I'll be all right." He got up and patted her shoulder as he passed her on his way out to finish the morning chores.

*   *   *

The *Parisian* had been sailing for eight days when Liam and Bobby came running to Liam's mother.

"Tá sé carraig bán mór," said Liam breathlessly, and Bobby added "Yes, a big white rock!" forgetting that Liam's mother needed no translator. Soon most of the passengers were on deck looking with wonder at a single white peak rising out of the water.

"It's an iceberg," said Mr. Langley to the boys near him. "You see, there are more coming up just ahead."

The sun shone off the dazzling white pieces of ice, in contrast to the dark water and the deep blue sky. Ned thought that he had never seen anything so beautiful. He wished he was an artist so that he could paint a picture of this scene and remember it always.

It was very cold on deck. The boys had been given heavy coats for their new life in Canada, but they and the other new clothes were locked away in the trunks in the hold of the ship. The steerage passengers were up and down the stairs a dozen times that day: up to look at the icebergs for as long as they could stand the cold, down again to get warm, and then back up on deck to gaze again.

"I wonder if I'll get put on a farm near my sister," said Dick as he rubbed his hands together and breathed on them to warm them. A fog had come rolling across the water, dimming the sun and making it even colder.

"Does she like it there?" asked Ned, trying to make out the shapes of the icebergs through the mist.

"I dunno. She wrote once just when she got there—she's helpin' a lady as has lots of children. Maybe she's too busy to write much."

Mr. Owen was passing them at that moment, and Dick said, "Excuse me, sir."

Mr. Owen paused and smiled at them. "Yes?"

"Is there rules about how often a chap can write to 'is family when 'e gets to Canada?"

"Bless me! As often as you like. Have you family that you would like to write to?"

"My sister is in 'Salt Steh Marie', sir, and I 'ave another sister still in England."

Mr. Owen cleared his throat to disguise the chuckle that he could not help.

"Oh, very near the American border, is she? Canadians say the name of that place 'Soo Saint Marie,' but I'll admit that 'Sault Ste Marie' written out looks the way you said it—to English people, at least."

"Then I may write to her as soon as I'm settled?"

"Of course! You'll be given two stamped postcards when you leave for your first situation and you may certainly use them to write to your family. And you?" he asked, turning to Ned. "Have you any family to write to?"

"No, sir."

"Well, well, never mind. Perhaps the family you go to will become like a family to you."

"Yes, sir," said Ned automatically, but the idea did not excite him. He hardly knew what a family was. Button-hole Row was not a place known for its domestic virtues, and he had seen much more kindness in the Home than he had ever seen in the few families he had known before going to Stepney.

Suddenly, the throbbing of the engines ceased, and the vibration they had grown accustomed to stopped.

"Is there summat wrong with the boat?" asked Ned. He did not much like the idea of drifting among icebergs for days, waiting to be rescued.

"No, no," said Mr. Owen. "We're nearing the shores of Newfoundland. You see how foggy it is; it's the ice fields that make the fog. We want to go slowly so as not to damage the boat by hitting one of the icebergs. Look closely, boys. You can sometimes see polar bear here."

The boys strained their eyes to look through the whiteness that surrounded the ship like a veil. Silently, the ship glided past icebergs of various sizes, but Ned saw no polar bears.

"Lookee there!" said Frank, whom Ned found at his side. "Look at them big white fish!" Ned looked down at the water and saw several large animals flanking the boat.

"They're whales—white whales," said Mr. Owen.

The pod of whales swam alongside the ship, coming to the surface now and then to breathe. Gracefully and effortlessly they skimmed along just under the surface. Ned watched them so intently that he was unaware that the murmurings of those around him were growing louder, and only when a shout went up did he look up and see what the noise was about: Land! There, through the mist, was the coastline of Newfoundland.

"We made it!" said Frank softly. Ned nodded and turned to remark that they had been seven days without seeing any land at all, but to his surprise, Frank's eyes were closed and he was whispering, "Thank You." Frank opened his eyes and saw Ned looking at him. He blushed, but a lopsided grin appeared before he turned away to look back out over the water.

When the ship had passed Belle Isle and come through the Strait safely, the engines were started again, and they sailed into the waters of the Gulf of St. Lawrence.

The next morning when the children were allowed to go on deck, a new spectacle met their eyes. From the shoreline to as far as the eye could see, a wilderness of trees decorated the banks. Many were bare, as spring had not yet come to put leaves on them, but there were a few evergreens as well—welcome colour to their eyes.

It was still too cold to stay on deck for long, but when they could they came up to gaze over the railings into the blue waters of the gulf. They turned a critical eye toward the other ships sailing near them (none so large as theirs, the boys were pleased to note) and watched the long island of Anticosti slip past them.

The evening meal was a noisy affair, the exuberance of their spirits overflowing and spilling out in their talk, their gestures, and their laughter: tomorrow they would land in Canada. In spite of the injunction to go to sleep quickly to get as much rest as they could before an early rising, more than one boy tossed and turned until the small hours.

At five o'clock in the morning, the boys were roused out of their beds and marched shivering onto the deck. Each carried his travelling bag. The stewards had been at work most of the night to bring all the trunks out of the hold and put them in rows across the deck. It was still dark, but each boy found his trunk, unlocked it with the key that had been put into its keyhole, and opened it for the first time. Quickly they changed into the new, warm clothes and hats and then put their travelling bags and their old clothes into the trunks, which were locked again. The boys sat on their trunks and watched the sun rise on the St. Lawrence River. There were fewer trees and hedges along the shore now; they had been cleared to make way for lots of white houses with red roofs.

At the sound of the signal, they went down for a final breakfast, and then came up again to watch the river grow narrower and the riverside more populated until they finally reached their destination: Point Levis, across the river from the city of Quebec.

Chapter 16

Ned shifted his body sleepily on the seat of the train as it rushed into the dawn. On the ship he had grown accustomed to sleeping on a moving bed, but it had been years since he'd had to sleep sitting up. His neck was sore from the unusual position of his head as he leaned against the window, and as the sunlight shined onto his face, he gave up the struggle to stay asleep. He let his eyes open and straightened himself up, stretching as well as he could in the small space he had.

The last twenty-four hours had been filled with bustle. After the ship had landed, the boys had disembarked and undergone an inspection by the Chief Medical Inspector, who checked for trachoma by turning back each boy's eyelid. Then their landing cards were stamped and Mr. Owen guided them to the passenger cars of a special train. They travelled along the southern shore of Quebec, through Richmond and into the sheds at Montreal for refuelling and boiled fresh eggs from local farms. Through the night the train clacked along past Belleville, Coburg, Port Hope, and northward.

Now the rising sun lit the farmland they were passing through. Ned was reminded of the train journey from London to Liverpool, but this land was very different. The fields were enormous, and vast tracts of woodland greeted his eyes. The buildings he saw were wooden, not stone or brick, and the train roared over bridges with rivers sparkling underneath. He might be sent to one of these farms. That one, maybe, with the white house.

Soon Mr. Owen came to tell Mr. Langley and the other escorts that Peterborough was just ahead, and there was a scramble to find missing caps and shoes; one pair of spectacles, after a frantic search by several people, was discovered in the owner's pocket. There was another great bustle getting off the train, and then finally they were walking the very short distance to "Hazelbrae," the new Barnardo home in Canada.

Hazelbrae had been built as a fine residence some forty years before and had recently been altered to include a three-storey addition on the back for a bathroom and dormitories. The drawing room had been converted to a play room, another large room was turned into a schoolroom, and the big kitchen was lined with enough tables to feed a hundred and fifty children. This would be the residence of children who were waiting for situations, of children who were ill and needed care, and of children who were moving from one placement to another. The boys who were now arriving would not be in the home for long. All of them were already spoken for, and most of them would leave the next day for their various farms.

While the boys were shown to the bedrooms and given lunch, Mr. Owen met with Mr. Duff, the superintendent of Hazelbrae, to see that all was in order.

"Have all the contracts been signed?"

"All but one. Mr. Foster, who applied for a boy, wrote a letter that we received two days ago, saying that he no longer needed help. Here is his letter."

Mr. Owen took the letter and read:

> Dear Sir,
>
> Since I wrote to you about getting a boy, I have had my troubles. We had a fire in the house and it burned down. I am staying with my brother now so there is no place to keep a boy. No more at present from
>
> Yours truly,
>
> J. Foster

"I see," said Mr. Owen.

"I looked over the applications that had come in after all the boys were assigned to see where the boy might be sent instead," said Mr. Duff. "I came across one case that seemed rather desperate." He picked up a piece of paper from the desk and looked it over. "Farmer and his wife with no children ... hired man with badly broken leg ... all the usual spring work to do ... already overworked ... would have sent in application sooner but was ill for several days ... hopes it is not too late."

"I'd say that was a good candidate. Any reason why the boy shouldn't be sent there?"

"The farmer asked for an older boy—it says here 'at least sixteen years old.' This boy, Edward Harrison, is only eleven. However, I thought that if he were to be placed with the farmer just until the next boatload of boys comes over, it might be some help."

"I agree. What has been done so far?"

"I sent a letter to this farmer—Johnson is his name—and explained the situation. There was no time to get a reply before the boys arrived, but I told him that I would escort Edward to Mount Forest station myself—I'm going anyway to escort little Bobby Tate to his adoptive parents—and we could discuss it then. If he agrees to take Edward for the time being, then he can sign the contract then and take the boy home with him; if not, I will bring Edward back with me and we will find another situation for him."

"You'll tell the boy that his place there will be only temporary, of course."

"Oh, yes. So long as Mr. Johnson and Edward both understand the circumstances, I think there will be no disappointed feelings."

*   *   *

It was a blow to Sam Johnson that the hoped-for youth would not be coming and a young boy was the best that could be had. He fretted a little over it, saying to his wife that if only he hadn't been ill and had been able to send the application in sooner, they might have gotten the help they needed. "I don't know as we ought to take this younger one," he said. "It might be more bother than anything."

"Oh, I don't know," said his wife. "Maybe he'll be big and strong for eleven. It's only for a few months. We'll make do. Any hands will be some help."

"He'll have to go to school if he's only eleven," Sam reminded her.

"Only for about two more months. He can work all summer."

She had her misgivings as well, but refused to think about them as she prepared one of the empty bedrooms for the boy. For the last week she had been thinking of a youth coming—one who was almost a man—and she had not thought his room would need any more arranging than Jake's room had. But somehow, knowing that it was a younger boy coming made a difference. She changed the dark blue curtains in the room with red ones from another room, put a nicer quilt on the bed than the one she had planned to use, and found a picture to put on the wall. She called Sam in to look at it when she was finished.

"Very nice," he said, smiling.

Martha was pleased to see the smile, glad that the cloud of discouragement and disappointment was beginning to lift, and that he was beginning to welcome the presence of a younger boy. In reality, Sam smiled because he was amused at his wife. He was quite sure that a boy, no matter what age, would not care about the colour of curtains or the patterns of quilts.

"He's coming in on the three o'clock?" asked Martha the next morning at breakfast.

"Yes," said Sam.

"We'll have a roast chicken for supper. I thought it would be a nice way to welcome him—poor boy, all alone in a strange land."

So Sam hitched up the wagon that afternoon and spent the five-mile drive to the train station trying again to reconcile himself to a strong eleven-year-old instead of a strong sixteen-year-old. By the time the train steamed into the station he was tolerably resigned, and he scanned the passengers stepping onto the platform for a man escorting a tall boy. Once, he thought he had found them, but this boy was too young—probably no more than nine. They seemed to be searching for someone, however, and to Sam's dismay, the man seemed to fix on him as a likely candidate and came over to him.

"Mr. Johnson?"

Sam nodded, trying to stifle the groan he felt welling up inside him.

"I see you received my letter. Will Ned here be any help to you for the next few months or would you rather wait for an older boy?"

Sam hesitated. Surely this boy could do nothing to help. He might even be in the way and create more work. It would probably be wiser to do without him and wait for an older boy. But then—there was Martha's labour in preparing the room and the supper cooking even now. The thought of Martha wasting her preparations, though a small thing, was enough to tip the balance.

"I'll take him," he said, rather grimly.

"Very well. If you would be so good as to sign this contract...we have a few moments, I believe, before the train moves on. Let us go into the station, where there will be a table and a pen. Ah, yes, porter, if you would please retrieve our trunk, thank you."

While the men went inside the station, Ned sat on his trunk and waited with a cold feeling in his stomach. This was every bit as bad has he had feared. He knew the farmer didn't really want him. Mr. Owen had explained that this was only a temporary situation, for a few months, until an older boy was available. Since they had left Peterborough he had seen several boys being met at the stations by the farmers they were going to help, and they had one and all been greeted, if not warmly, at least cordially. He had imagined the same thing for himself.

Mr. Owen and Mr. Johnson came out of the station and shook hands.

"Goodbye, Ned," said Mr. Owen, turning to him. "God be with you. I will see you in a few months." He laid a friendly hand on Ned's shoulder and then boarded the train again. Bobby, who was going still further, waved his hand to Ned, and Ned waved back.

"Well, let's be going," said Mr. Johnson. He picked up Ned's trunk and led the way to the wagon. Ned clambered up onto the wagon seat and began the journey to the farm that didn't really want him.

Chapter 17

The first mile to Ned's new home was travelled in near-misery. Every moment that passed was taking him further from everything he knew. The last two weeks had separated him from all familiar surroundings, but now he was separated from all familiar people as well. His future was uncertain. '*Yea, though I walk through the valley of the shadow of death,*' he thought, and then smiled a little at himself. To call his situation "the valley of the shadow of death" was probably an exaggeration. *In any case,* he remembered, '*Thou art with me.*'

At first the landscape passed before his eyes unseen, but now he began to notice things. He had never seen countryside before leaving London two weeks ago, and the farmland he had glimpsed from the train in the last few days had been observed at considerable speed. Now he could look carefully as the wagon went along the road.

They passed farmers mending fences and cows looking forlornly at the barren earth, waiting for the first grass of spring. They passed groves of trees, large fields, and big wooden barns. The farmhouses were magnificent—large, two-storey homes with porches in front. Ned had never seen houses like them. Birds flew overhead and rabbits disappeared into the fields by the side of the road as the wagon approached.

Sam was silent for the first part of the journey. His disappointment began to turn into frustration—what *would* he do with all the spring work and only this little boy to help? And what if this boy was a difficult child? He might be sulky and refuse to work at all. He had still said nothing, after all.

He glanced at Ned, who was wholly absorbed in watching the passing scenery. Suddenly, Ned turned to Sam and said, "What do they call them fences, sir? The ones with the big sticks that go back and forth?" He pointed to one in the distance.

"Those are split-rail snake fences," replied Sam, amused at the boy's accent. It was strange to hear a child pronounce the words so differently. Now that an opening was made, he might as well ask the boy a few questions.

"Have you ever milked a cow, Ned?"

"No, sir." Ned felt wretchedly guilty as he made this admission.

"Well, I suppose you can learn," said Sam.

"Yessir," said Ned.

"Have you even been on a farm before?"

"No, sir. I never left London until two weeks ago."

"Ever chop wood?"

"No, sir." Ned's head bowed in shame. "We burned coal in our fires. I can fetch coal..."

A little bit of sympathy stirred Sam's heart. Ned would probably be no help at all, but he seemed eager enough to please, and after all, it wasn't his fault he knew nothing about farm work.

"Never mind," said Sam. "I'll teach you what you need to know, and then you'll be all ready for the next farm you go to."

"Yessir," said Ned, brightening a little. Perhaps if he learned well at the Johnson farm, then the next farm he was sent to would be glad he had come.

At last the wagon turned off the road and they drove around to the back of a farmhouse, causing chickens to scatter out of the way, clucking indignantly.

"Here we are," said Sam as he stopped the horses. A large dog came racing around the side of the house, barking madly.

"That's enough, Digger," said Sam. Ned climbed down from the wagon and the dog sniffed him eagerly, wagging his tail all the while. Ned gingerly patted the dog's head. He watched as Sam effortlessly shouldered the trunk and went into the house. Ned hoped he was doing the right thing by following; for all he knew Mr. Johnson was expecting him to do something with the horses—heaven only knew what.

He followed Mr. Johnson through a little room with boots on the floor and coats hung on the wall, and into a kitchen.

"Well, here he is, Martha," said Sam as his wife came into the kitchen.

"So you're Edward," she said with a smile.

"Ned," corrected Sam. "You're called Ned, aren't you?"

Ned nodded. "Yes, sir." A little of Ned's apprehension was relieved. Mrs. Johnson looked like she wanted him.

"Welcome," she said. "I'll show you your bedroom."

She led him up the stairs and down a hall and then ushered him in to his room. It was not large, but there was a wooden bedstead with a plump mattress covered with a quilt and to the side was a wooden chest of drawers. It was clean and tidy and colourful. Ned had never seen such a bedroom. Katie's room had only had a pile of rags for a bed. The Barnardo Home had proper beds, of course, but the dormitory had an institutional look. This bedroom was far beyond anything he'd imagined.

Mr. Johnson put the trunk down in the corner of the room and said, "Well, Ned, we'd best be going out to care for the horses."

*　　　*　　　*

That night Ned lay in bed, waiting for sleep to come. He remembered his first night at the Home four years ago and how frightened he had been. But then he'd had Jack and now he had no one. For the first time he was really alone. At the Home, the other boys had been similar to himself and the ways of the Home were quickly learned. The songs and the schoolwork were the same as at the Ragged School, and he was still in a city. He had thought at the time that it was all so very different from his former life, but he could see now that it wasn't.

Here, every single thing was new. The animals were large and frightening. The work was unknown. He knew no one. Mr. and Mrs. Johnson were kind, especially Mrs. Johnson, but they were strangers. And he had been hoping that even though it was new, it would be his settled home. Instead, it seemed like he would learn the ways here and then go off to a new place again.

Deliberately, he whispered his favourite hymn to himself:

> Though it be the gloom of night,
> Though we see no ray of light,

Since the Lord Himself is there

'Tis not meet that we should fear.

It don't seem true, though, thought Ned. *It don't seem that the Lord Himself is here. I feel all alone—I am all alone.* He was struck with a pang of nostalgia. If he were back at the Home, now, there would have been no loneliness at all: just the pleasant, frank conversation of comrades. It was only this morning that he had said goodbye to them—just a wave of the hand as they left Hazelbrae to meet a different train than his. He would probably never see them again. He missed Dick, perhaps, more than anyone. Dick always knew what to say when there was some spiritual difficulty. He imagined himself saying to Dick, "Dick, I ain't sure that the Lord is here. It don't feel like He is." And then he knew what Dick would say: "That don't mean He isn't. Truth don't always *feel* true, but it is."

Ned nodded his head in agreement with the imaginary Dick, and then whispered all the other verses of the hymn to himself. It did him a great deal of good.

*   *   *

"Well, what do you think?" said Sam to his wife after Ned had gone to bed that night. They were sitting in the kitchen; Martha was knitting a pair of socks and Sam was looking over the latest edition of the *Family Herald.*

"He's small for eleven years old, isn't he?"

"He is."

"Was he any help?"

"Not much. He did what he was told, and I will say that he made an effort. It's just that he's not used to any of this work. Why, when I was eleven I could chop the wood, harness the horses, milk the cows...Ned couldn't even bring the cows in from the field without help. I sent him to get them and Maisy bellowed at him—you know how she does—and he turned tail and ran." Sam chuckled. "I was surprised at how fast he could run. He said he'd never seen a cow before, except from the train window."

"He'll do better at that tomorrow."

Sam shook his head. "I think it will snow tonight. The cows will be in for a little while."

"I suppose you'll just have to keep him with you until he gets used to it all."

Sam sighed. "Yes. Only it means that everything takes twice as long."

They were both silent a moment, thinking. Suddenly Martha said, "I like him."

Sam smiled at her. "I must say, I like him, too. He'll be a good little helper for the next farmer that gets him. I only wish..." His voice trailed off. It was useless to say again that he wished Ned was older.

"Do we have to send him to school tomorrow?"

"I think not. He's only just arrived. And if it snows tonight and is clear tomorrow, we'll have a day in the sugar bush. I missed some good days when I was sick."

Martha nodded.

"At least there's a sugar shack for you to stay in while you watch the sap boiling," Sam went on. "It'll be warmer for you."

"I'm all right," said Martha. "I can bear the cold as well as you can."

"You shouldn't have to," mumbled Sam. If there had been an able-bodied man to help, Martha would not have to go out and help make maple syrup.

"Never mind," she said. "It's the middle of April—there won't be much sap running after this anyway."

"True enough," said Sam. "It's been a rather mild spring."

"And Ned will be a help, I'm sure," pursued Martha, "even if he's never done it before."

"We'll see," said Sam. "At any rate, we'll bring him along and hope he stays out of mischief."

Chapter 18

The next morning, Ned awakened to a knock on his door. It was five o'clock in the morning, and still dark. Groggily he got up and pulled on his warm clothes. He took his boots in his hand and walked down the stairs with them into the kitchen. Martha was putting more wood into the cook stove and Sam was in the little room off the kitchen where the boots and outerwear were kept; he was putting on his coat and hat. Ned got his feet into his boots. He had not worn them before; they came up to his calves and felt stiff. He put on a coat, hat, and gloves and followed the farmer out into a white world. Snow had fallen in the night, blanketing the earth. The black of night was slowly giving way to the grey that comes before the dawn. The snow came up to the top of his boots, though it did not go into them because his trousers came down over the boots. He tried to follow in the footprints Mr. Johnson made, but he couldn't quite do it—they were too far apart. Digger frisked alongside him as if a romp in the snow before dawn was the only way to start the day.

Martha watched them from the kitchen window and wondered how long it would take Ned to learn to milk a cow. It was her habit to pray about seemingly small matters and she prayed now that Ned would learn quickly. She watched until they disappeared into the barn, and then went up to Ned's bedroom. To her surprise, Ned's bed was made as neatly as she would have made it and his nightclothes were nowhere to be seen. She peeped into his trunk and saw them there, nicely folded. "Well, think of that!" she said aloud, and went back downstairs to make breakfast.

When Sam and Ned came in, they were grinning.

"Ned got a little milk out of Bluebell," said Sam.

"Well done, Ned," said Martha warmly. "Sit down and eat before it's cold."

They sat down and Sam and Martha bowed their heads to say grace. Ned was caught off guard again. It had seemed very odd yesterday that they did not sing the grace as he had always done in the Ragged School, the Home, and on board the ship. He was not sure it was right to eat if he had not *sung* the grace. And it had seemed ungrateful to leave the table without singing the grace after meals.

Ned had never seen such a breakfast. For the last few years he had been given porridge every day for his morning meal. There was porridge here, too (with cream!), but also eggs, bacon, and bread. Ned ate everything on his plate and was surprised when Martha offered him *another* egg. He took it with so much gratitude that Sam and Martha began to think it not so very strange that he was small in stature. After breakfast, Ned cleared the plates from the table without prompting. The Johnsons looked at him in surprise; in their experience, boys did not clear tables. They did not stop him, however.

Sam got up from the table. "Since today is Friday, I think we'll wait until Monday to send you to school. I need help in the sugar bush. You'll be ready to come, Martha, after we finish in the barn?"

Martha nodded and man and boy went back out to the barn. Ned wondered exactly what a "sugar bush" was and what they were going to do with it. He had learned in school that sugar came from sugar cane, which was grown in the West Indies. Was the sugar bush a plant that made a different kind of sugar? Mr. Johnson seemed too keen to get the work in the barn finished for Ned to be comfortable asking questions, so he kept quiet and worked as well as he could. Just as they had finished pitching down hay for the cattle, the barn door opened and in stepped a youth with red hair poking out from under his hat.

"Hello, Sam!" he called out.

"Hello, George!" said Sam. "What are you doing here?"

George grinned. "Dad was going to have me mend fences today, but the snow put an end to that plan. He thought you might need help in the bush, so I came along to see if you wanted me."

"I do want you. We're nearly finished here. Go tell your sister we don't need her to come with us after all. No, wait—Ned, you go and tell Mrs. Johnson she doesn't need to come. Tell her we'll be ready for our dinner at twelve. George, you get Clover and Billy and hitch them up to the sleigh."

Ned put the pitchfork he had been using back in its place and followed his own tracks back to the house. Martha was just taking off her apron as Ned entered the kitchen.

"Excuse me, missus," he said, "But Mr. Johnson says that George is here an' you don't need to come after all. Oh! An' he says we'll ready for the dinner at twelve."

Martha laughed. "He needn't tell me. If he ever wants dinner later than the stroke of noon, I'll know the world has stopped turning. Well! This means I can bake the bread after all."

Ned went back outside where the sleigh was being loaded with a large barrel and some empty pails. He looked at the tree standing near the house and marvelled at the layer of snow, like icing, that frosted the top of every twig and branch. He reached down and scooped up a handful of the soft whiteness. It stuck to his gloves.

"Ever seen snow before?" asked George.

"Yes," said Ned. "It snowed in London now and then, but it weren't like this. It got mucky before long an' it melted pretty quick."

The three of them sat down on the sleigh, and the horse pulled them across a snow-covered field to the trees all huddled together and covering (if Ned had been able to calculate it) about twelve acres. Digger trotted along behind them.

"Is it *your* forest?" asked Ned, and George chuckled.

"It's only Sam's woodlot. We call it the sugar bush when we're making syrup. Some of the trees are maple trees that we use for making syrup and sugar; the other trees are used for building and burning."

"Oh," said Ned.

They entered the woodlot. Many of the trees seemed to have a stick poking out of their sides and a bucket hanging under the stick. But Ned was not close enough to see exactly what it was like. The horse pulled the sleigh to a small wooden building.

"This is the sugar shack," said George.

It truly was a shack. On one side of the single room, wood was stacked against the wall. On the dirt floor were two arrangements of stones and the charred remains of fires. On top of each fire-place was a huge kettle, hanging from a rough pole that was supported by a forked branch on each side. Old, mismatched chairs stood about.

"I'll open the roof, shall I?" asked George.

"Yes, do," said Sam.

Then Ned noticed that some of the boards of the roof could be taken off.

It must be to let the smoke out, thought Ned.

"We'll need more wood," said Sam. "George, you stay here and chop some while Ned and I start getting the sap."

George began taking logs outside to the chopping block and Sam led the way back out to the sleigh.

"Come on, Ned," said Sam. "We'll start over here." He walked the horse on as he explained. "The sap runs out of the trees through the spiles and down into the buckets. You need to empty each bucket into your pail until it is full, or—" as he looked at Ned's arms—"until it is as heavy as you can carry. Then empty your pail into the barrel on the sleigh. When it is full, we will take it back to the sugar shack and George will boil it down. Now, here's where we start."

Ned took a pail and went to the nearest tree. Something that looked like water was dripping out of the spile into the bucket, which was only about one-third full. He carefully poured the sap into his pail and replaced the bucket. The tree next to it did not have a spile and bucket—evidently it was another kind of tree. He found another maple, and emptied that bucket. The snow crunched under his boots as he walked from tree to tree, and the sun sparkled off the snow and dazzled his eyes. After emptying several buckets, his pail was very heavy. He brought it over to the sleigh and poured the sap into the barrel. He wondered how many buckets he had emptied into his pail before it became too heavy; he would count next time. One... two...

three... four... five... six—ugh, it was heavy! Seven... eight... no more. He could barely struggle with it to the sleigh.

Digger amused himself by chasing squirrels and running around following rabbit tracks. Whenever he came near, Ned gave him a pat. When all the trees around the sleigh had been seen to, Sam moved the sleigh on to a new area. As Sam filled his own pail time and time again, he kept an eye on Ned. He noticed that the boy did not complain or dawdle, even though he was tired and certainly wasn't used to walking in snow. After an hour and a half, he called to Ned to get onto the sleigh. Ned's arms were sore and his hands were cold and his feet were freezing, though the rest of his body was warm from the exercise.

At the sugar shack, there was a fire going and all three workers used the pails to transfer the sap from the barrel to the kettles. Then Sam and Ned sat down on the chairs and rested and warmed themselves by the fire. The bottoms of their trousers were soaked from wading through the wet snow.

"How long does it have to boil for?" asked Ned.

"Oh, this kettle will need to boil for seven hours or so before the sap is completely turned into syrup," said Sam. "It takes about forty gallons of sap to make one gallon of syrup."

"And what do you use the syrup for?" asked Ned.

George laughed. "You mean you've never had maple syrup on your pancakes?"

"No," said Ned. He did not like to admit that he did not know what pancakes were.

"We make some of it into sugar, too," volunteered George. If you boil the syrup long enough it turns into sugar."

"Oh," said Ned.

"We'll probably have pancakes for breakfast one of these days," said Sam, "and you'll be able to try the syrup on them."

Ned nodded and watched the fire. It crackled and glowed in a very cheerful way. The smell of burning wood was very different to the smell of coal-fire smoke. Ned thought it was more pleasant. He looked at the stack of wood that George had chopped in their absence; it seemed like a large amount. Ned shrank from the idea of what would have happened if Mr. Johnson had asked *him* to chop the wood. He'd never tried to chop wood. Probably he could have chopped a little bit, but nothing like what was needed. Of course, George was older; he was probably around sixteen years old. Still, it seemed impossible to Ned that he would ever be strong enough to really help around this farm.

They sat for a few more minutes before Sam decided that it was time to go out again. They worked for another hour and a half, Ned growing more weary all the time, and then it was back to the sugar shack for another rest. The new sap was put into another barrel to wait until the kettles were ready for more sap.

Sam pulled out his watch. "Twelve o'clock," he announced with satisfaction. "Martha will be here soon." He reached over to get a long-handled ladle and dipped it into the bubbling kettle. He drank from the ladle and then passed it to George. George took a drink and gave a sigh of satisfaction. Sam dipped it in again and gave the ladle to Ned. Ned sipped the hot sap; it was sweet and delicious. He thought it was the nicest drink he had had in his life.

"I wonder how Dad's getting on," said George. "He thought one of the cows would calve today. Young cow—her first calf."

Sam smiled at his brother-in-law. "You always liked the baby animals, didn't you, George?"

"Aw, well," grinned George. "I suppose that's true enough. It's come in handy for Dad, too, sometimes. Remember that litter of pigs I nursed through when the sow died? Dad gave me half the money he made from selling them. He said he'd have lost them all if it weren't for me."

"And what did you buy with all that wealth?"

"Nothing. I'm saving it."

"Wise man," said Sam and looked at his watch again. "It's odd Martha's not here yet. Maybe I'll take a look and see if she's coming." He went outside.

Ned watched George skim the foam off the boiling sap. "It gets the impurities out," George explained.

Ten minutes later Sam came in to say that there was no sign of Martha and that he would go back to the farm and see what the trouble was. Ned was thankful that he could stay and rest in the sugar shack for a little while longer.

The boys sat in silence for a few minutes and then George said, "Do you like Canada?"

"I dunno," said Ned. "It's so different. But I get lots o' food here. I think I'll like it after a time."

George looked at Ned as if he were evaluating his merits and then nodded twice to himself.

"You'll do," he said.

"Do what?" asked Ned.

"Oh, I mean you'll do well at farming when you're used to it. You've got the right look about you."

"Do I?"

"Oh, yes," said George with an air of authority.

"I didn't 'specially *want* to be a farmer," said Ned doubtfully.

"You'll do well all the same," said George and was silent for a few minutes. Then he said, "Tell me about the ship you came over on. Was it large?"

So Ned told him all about the journey by steamship, and received the impression that George rather envied him for having travelled on such a large ship and having survived such a terrifying storm at sea. Ned was just describing the icebergs and whales when Sam appeared again carrying a basket.

"Martha's sprained her ankle rather badly," he said with a sigh. "She was standing on a chair to reach a basket on the high shelf when she lost her balance and came down the wrong way on her foot. I got her in bed and put snow on her ankle, but she won't be doing much for a few days. I brought the food—she kept on fixing it even after she hurt herself." He paused to shake his head at her perseverance in working even when she was hurt. No doubt she had made her injury worse, but he was rather proud of her all the same. "After you eat, Ned, go back to the house and Mrs. Johnson will tell you what to do to help her around the house. George and I will carry on here."

In the basket were cups, plates, forks, and knives, along with one dish of baked beans, one of fried chicken, and some sliced bread, already buttered. Sam dished the food onto the plates, thanked God for the food, and put hot sap into the cups for them to drink with the meal. Ned felt very full as he took the basket and followed the tracks left in the snow back all the way to the house.

Chapter 19

Martha sat propped up with pillows on her bed, her hands busy with knitting and her foot wrapped in a towel and resting in a pan of snow. *I ought to be sitting down in the kitchen*, she thought. *At least then I could keep a watch on things and give instructions to the boy about making supper. Perhaps I could hobble down on my own without waiting for Sam.* She unwrapped her ankle from the towel and saw that it was swollen and purple. Shaking her head, she wrapped it up again and resigned herself to an afternoon of sitting still. She could hear the boy coming up the stairs now in his woollen-stockinged feet. Thank goodness he had remembered to take his boots off before coming through the house.

"Come in here, please," she called.

Ned came in with his cap in his hand, diffident and respectful. He rather reminded Martha of one of her little brothers—one who had died in childhood. He, too, had had a wistful look in his eyes, and a hesitation that came from wanting to avoid making mistakes.

"How did you get on in the bush?" she asked.

"Very well, missus," said Ned.

"Are you tired?"

"No, ma'am. Well, yes, ma'am, but not so tired as I couldn't do more."

Martha smiled at him. "It's hard work, I know. Now, I've been thinking that you might be able to make some soup if I tell you what to do. You seem to be good at following instructions."

"Yes, missus," said Ned, "I'll do my best."

"Well, it will be a help even if you can't finish it all yourself. All right then, go down to the cold cellar and get the plate of chicken on the shelf by the stairs. And you can get a couple carrots and potatoes and onions, too. Bring them all up to the kitchen, and then come back here and I will tell you what to do with them."

"Yes, ma'am."

Ned went down to the kitchen. "The cold cellar," he murmured to himself. Vaguely he remembered that last night Mrs. Johnson had opened a trap door in the floor—over there somewhere—and disappeared down some steps. He went over to the place and found the handle. With a mighty heave, he opened the door. Stairs went down into the darkness. He hoped that light from the kitchen would shine down there enough for him to see what he was doing. He would rather not hunt for candles and matches in a house where he was still nearly a stranger.

He descended into the cellar. It *was* cold—colder than he expected. There was enough light for him to see a shelf near to the stairs and the plate of chicken on it. He brought that up carefully and set it on the kitchen table. Then he went back down. Where would the vegetables be? He looked around in the gloom and saw baskets sitting on the floor. He went over and peered into them. They were not full, but there appeared to be things in them. He reached into one and pulled out something round and hard—a potato? He took it over to the steps where there was more light. Yes, it was a potato. He went back for a couple more, and then tried another basket, and another. Carrots, onions, parsnips—that would do. He brought them all up to the kitchen table and closed the trap door. Then he went to report to Mrs. Johnson.

"I found the chicken and them vegetables, missus," said Ned. "It was cold in the cellar, all right."

"Well done," said Martha. "Yes, it is cold. We put snow along one side and cover it with straw, and, being below ground, it keeps the cellar cold all summer. Now listen carefully. You must chop up the chicken and be sure there are no bones. Then put the chicken in the kettle that's sitting on the floor near the stove. And then peel the vegetables—oh! I don't suppose you know how to do that. Well, you must do what you can. Take the small knife and scrape away the dark skins of the potatoes and the outside of the carrots and then chop up all the vegetables into little pieces. Do you think you can do that?"

Ned wanted to laugh. Mrs. Johnson obviously did not know that he had peeled and chopped vegetables every week for the last four years. But he only smiled and said, "Yes, missus, I can do that."

"Very well. Then you must put enough water into the kettle to cover the chicken and vegetables and put a little salt in and then put the lid on the kettle. Put the kettle on top of the stove and leave it to cook. I wish I'd gotten the bread made, but it can't be helped."

A thought sprang into Ned's mind: couldn't he make the bread? He had never made one loaf from beginning to end, but he was confident that he could do it. He opened his mouth to say something about it, but then closed it again. Perhaps Canadian ingredients were different or he couldn't do it after all. Best to say nothing until he knew it could be done.

"Do I need to add more wood to the stove, missus? I ain't done that before. We only had coal fires in England."

"No, Mr. Johnson fixed up the stove before he left with the food. It should be all right for now."

Downstairs, Ned surveyed the kitchen. The dry ingredients for the bread had already been measured and were sitting in a bowl on a small table next to the wall. He would finish the bread first and then make the soup. It took him a few minutes to find the butter and milk and to get the water warm, but once the dough had been made it was easy work—in fact, almost mindless—to knead the dough and set it to rise near the stove. Then he chopped the chicken, peeled and diced the vegetables and put them all in the pot with salt and water, leaving it on the stove to simmer.

Then he went back upstairs and reported that the soup was made. Martha was tempted to ask him to repeat back to her everything he had done in the kitchen, but stopped herself. She remembered that her own younger brothers found nothing so wearying as being catechised about how they had done their work. She would let it go and hope for the best.

"Now then," she said. "I wonder what else you could do."

"I could sweep the kitchen floor, ma'am," Ned said. "It seems to want sweeping."

"Well, yes, I suppose you might do that. There's a broom in the corner by the cold cellar."

Ned found the broom and swept the floor. Then he thought that he might as well wash the dirty dishes and cups that were still in the basket as well as the used pans and bowls scattered around the kitchen. He heated water on the stove, found the washing pan and filled it, and scrubbed them all.

Martha used up her ball of yarn and began to wonder why it was taking so long for Ned to sweep the kitchen. Was he ruining anything? It was frustrating to be upstairs doing nothing while an inexperienced boy tried to run her kitchen. She wondered if he had managed to cut up the vegetables and chicken all right. A little sister of hers had once been instructed to cut the potatoes into bite-sized pieces. She had tried, but when the soup was handed around at supper, one of her brothers had quipped that the potatoes were bite-sized, all right—for a mule. She could hear dishes rattling downstairs now, and it unnerved her. Perhaps it was best to risk the ankle and make sure everything was well. And she was sure she could finish making the bread sitting down.

Ned was stacking the dry dishes and humming "Forth in Thy Name, O Lord" when he heard a shuffling noise from overhead. Then came rather loud thumping sounds. Wondering if Mrs. Johnson was trying to get his attention, he went quickly to the stairs and looked up to see her limping—almost hopping—to the head of the stairs.

"Can I help you, missus?" asked Ned, going up to meet her.

"Yes, you can let me lean on you a little as I go down the stairs. I suppose it is rather foolish of me to try—ow!" she said as she made her hazardous way down. "But I was out of yarn and the snow was melted and it seemed silly for me to be lying there in the middle of the day while you struggled to do the work in the kitchen. I thought perhaps I could finish making the bread if I sat on a chair..." They reached the bottom in safety, and Ned gave her his arm as she hobbled along to the kitchen. He pulled out a chair for her and she sat down heavily.

"Thank you, Ned. Now, if you will get me the things I need for making the bread, I will see to that. You could fetch the pan I left upstairs and get it full of snow; that way I could be doing something for my ankle..." she paused as she caught sight of the stacked crockery. "Are all those dishes clean?"

"Yes, ma'am. I thought I might as well wash them."

"Oh!" said Martha. "Thank you. That was very thoughtful." *I hope they really are clean*, she added to herself. *But I suppose even to have them rinsed off would make things easier.*

"Now, about the bread," she went on aloud, and then looked around, puzzled. "Why, I thought I left the bowl of flour there on the table."

"You did, missus. I finished makin' the dough an' then I put it on to rise. I think it's near ready to put in the pans." So saying, he got the bowl of rising dough and lifted the cloth. "Yes, missus, it's ready. If you tell me where your bread pans is I'll get it ready for the second risin'."

Martha stared at him for a full ten seconds, astonished beyond speech. Ned began to be uncomfortable. Had he done wrong?

"I'm sorry, missus," he ventured. "I thought maybe you'd like it if I made the bread."

Martha recovered herself. "My word!" she said. "I had no idea you could do that! Of course I like it. You just took me by surprise is all. The bread pans are on the bottom shelf there."

Ned got the pans and greased them with butter and then punched down the dough, shaped it, and put it in the pans. He covered them and put them back near the stove to rise.

"Did your mother teach you that?" said Martha, who had watched him in stupefied silence.

"No. I never knew my mum. They taught us to bake at the Home."

"Oh. Were you orphaned, then?"

Ned shrugged. "Dunno. I don't know where I come from. I only remember being in Button-hole Row—that was the name of our alley—and the ladies gave me bits o' food and let me sleep on their floors sometimes."

"You never had a mother," Martha mused. "And no family." She could hardly imagine such a circumstance. She had been raised in a large family with many siblings and living close by to aunts, uncles, cousins, and grandparents. It seemed so unnatural: this boy living his life without a mother, she living her life without a child.

"Did you ever wish you had a family?" she asked.

"No," said Ned, thinking back. "Not really. Most of the families I knew weren't nothin' to boast on. Except Katie's mum. Katie's mum was a nice lady, like you." Martha's face flushed a little at this compliment. "I wouldn't 'ave minded belonging to her. But it weren't hardly a family—just the two of 'em."

At half past four, Sam came back to do the afternoon milking, leaving George in the sugar bush to watch the boiling sap. He grinned when he saw Martha down in the kitchen instead of up in her bed. He'd had very little hope that she would stay put when there was work to be done.

"How is it coming along?" asked Martha.

"I think we'll be finished by midnight," said Sam. "I'll do the milking and eat and then send George back for some food. Where's Ned?"

"He's upstairs getting my mending basket."

"You've been busy enough, I should think," said Sam. "I see you've been making soup and baking bread and who knows what all instead of resting your ankle."

"I didn't," said Martha. "Ned did it all."

"Well, you're a wonder for giving directions, then. I'm glad you could do that from your chair."

"No, you don't understand," said Martha. "Ned did it without my directions. Apparently he's been making bread, chopping vegetables, washing dishes and doing all sorts of housework for the last few years. He didn't need any help."

Sam gave a long, low whistle, and then broke into a chuckle. "It seems that we asked for a hired boy and got a housekeeper instead. Perhaps if we'd asked for a girl, they would have sent us a lumberjack."

"Now, Sam! Do you know that he didn't know a blessed thing except how to carry parcels for strangers until he went to that Home four years ago? I've been sitting here thinking it's a blessing we'll have him for a few months. If he can learn all that and do so well at it, don't you think he can learn to do farm work just as well?"

"Well, there's something in that. He does work hard—no slacking."

"None. He did far more than I asked him to."

They heard Ned coming down the stairs then, and the conversation ended. But as Sam and Ned worked together to milk the cows, the discussion came back to Sam's mind: *Don't you think he can learn to do farm work just as well?...Well, there's something in that. He does work hard—no slacking...None. He did far more than I asked him to.*

"There's something in that," he murmured to himself. "There's something in that. Or maybe—there's something in *him*."

Chapter 20

August, 1884

T hough it was only morning, the little office at Hazelbrae was already very warm as Mr. Duff dealt with the daily mail. Two tradesmen's bills were taken care of, a letter of enquiry was answered, likewise also one letter of thanks from the adoptive parents of little Bobby, and then there was one that darkened his usually placid face and brought out worry-wrinkles on his brow.

"Good morning, Duff," said Mr. Owen, coming in without knocking and dropping into a chair with a smile. "Shockingly hot already, isn't it? Like an oven. I say, what's the trouble?"

Mr. Duff handed the letter to Mr. Owen, saying, "It's another one."

Mr. Owen took the letter and read:

"Dear Sirs,

I am the Methodist minister in Teeswater. Your organization placed a boy, Ralph Shaw, at the farm of John Webster near my home. This boy has been mistreated since the day he arrived at that farm two years ago. He is now sixteen years old. We have watched him labour from morning till night without proper food or clothing. He is whipped for the slightest offence. He has been constantly insulted and harshly spoken to, and he has never been paid the wages that were due him. Until recently, he has been allowed to attend church, but now he has been forbidden even that. It is to his credit that he has never returned evil for evil, but at last he was driven to escape. He came to my house last evening and begged me to take him in. The purple bruise on his face where the farmer hit him was ample reason for me to grant his request. I would keep him myself, but really have no use for a boy. Therefore, I ask that you send someone to come and get him. And please do try to find a better situation for him.

Yours sincerely,
Rev. H. A. Fischer

While Mr. Owen was reading the letter, Mr. Duff looked through his files and found the one for Ralph Shaw. He was paging through it when Mr. Owen looked up.

"Was the Webster home ever visited?"

"Yes, once. It says here that the visitor spoke with the farmer who said that all was going well, and the boy Ralph said nothing to contradict him. Another visit was scheduled for next month."

Mr. Owen gave a long sigh. "He's the fifth one we've heard about, isn't he?"

"Yes, the fifth one of *ours*."

Mr. Owen nodded. They had heard of plenty of cases of abuse with other child emigrant organizations, but had been hoping that their children would be better protected. Both men sat in silence, feeling helpless. They knew that there were probably many more cases of maltreatment that had not been reported. Mr. Duff drummed his fingers on the desk and looked out the window; Mr. Owen re-read the letter until he could have recited it from memory.

"Could we arrange for more farm visits?" asked Mr. Duff.

Mr. Owen shook his head. "We don't have the funds to pay more visitors, and the ones we have are busier than they ought to be—as you know."

"Yes. And if we reduce the number of emigrants, then the Homes in Britain will overflow, and they may have to start turning children away..."

"...And the children on the streets will be as badly off as ever," finished Mr. Owen. "It's difficult to know what we could be doing differently." He looked again at the letter and heaved another sigh. "Well, there's nothing to do but to take him away. It will not be hard to find him another place. I seem to remember promising a farmer out that way that I would find an older boy for him—yes, that's right—I left a younger boy with him until the next group of boys would come. I'm sure he'd take Ralph, and I can bring the younger boy back here until we find a farm for him. I'll look over my notes and see who it was."

He did so, and was delighted to discover that the farmer who wanted an older boy was a Mr. Johnson, living near Mount Forest, which was a mere two railway stops before Teeswater. He could go to the Johnson farm and discuss the matter with them on the way. If Mr. Johnson was agreeable, Mr. Owen could then travel on to Teeswater and get Ralph, deliver him to the Johnsons, and collect the younger boy and bring him back to Hazelbrae. A very neat and efficient arrangement. He made plans to go the next morning.

*   *   *

Jake, the hired man, was digging potatoes when a buggy turned into the farmyard. He recognized it as one of the buggies for hire that could be obtained in Mount Forest. He walked slowly, still limping slightly, to meet it. The man driving the buggy was not a farmer, but a city man, with a bowler hat and well-shined shoes. He called out, "Is this the Johnson farm?"

"Yep," said Jake.

"Are you Mr. Johnson?"

"No."

The man's eyes looked him over, but not unkindly. "Hired man?" he asked.

"Yep."

"Is Mr. Johnson about?"

"He's in the field, looking at the wheat. It's nearly dinner time, though. He'll be in soon."

The man got out of the buggy and fanned himself with his hat. "My name's Owen," he said. "I'm from the Barnardo Home in Peterborough." He stopped fanning and looked at Jake. "You weren't here in the spring, were you?"

"No. I'd broke my leg and went to my sister's while it mended. I've only been back these last two weeks."

"Ah," said Mr. Owen. "It must have been a difficult time for the Johnsons when you were laid up."

"It was that."

"Yes. Mr. Johnson asked me for an older boy to help, but the only lad available was a young boy called Edward—Ned. I promised I'd be back in the autumn to exchange the younger boy for an older one."

Jake chuckled. "Is that so?"

Mr. Owen wondered what the joke was, but answered mildly, "Yes, that's so."

"Ned's in the house, helping Mrs. Johnson clean out the cold cellar. Would you like to see him? I'll get him for you. Oh, and there's Mr. Johnson coming." Jake moved off toward the house, and Mr. Owen approached Sam with an outstretched hand.

"Hello, Mr. Johnson. I'm Mr. Owen from the Barnardo Home."

"Oh, yes, of course," said Sam, shaking the offered hand.

"I have good news for you. I've found you an older boy. I didn't forget, you see. There's a boy of sixteen that needs a new situation, and he's over in Teeswater. I can get him this afternoon and bring him here, and if Ned can be ready to go then, I'll bring him back to Hazelbrae with me."

Martha and Ned came out of the house together and walked over to the men.

"Martha, Ned," said Sam, "This is Mr. Owen from the Barnardo Home."

Martha acknowledged the introduction with a nod and Ned soberly shook Mr. Owen's hand. It had come, then. The day he had been dreading.

"I can see you've grown, Ned," said Mr. Owen. "Farm life must agree with you."

"Yessir," said Ned quietly.

"Now then, Martha," said Sam. "Mr. Owen says that he can take Ned away and bring us an older boy."

"Oh!" said Martha in a changed voice and unconsciously put her hand on Ned's shoulder. "When?"

"Today," said Mr. Owen, and Ned felt Martha's hand grip his shoulder more tightly. "I could go and get the other boy and bring him back here this afternoon, and then Ned could come back with me to the Home."

The question of whether or not to keep Ned had been turning itself over in Sam's mind all summer. At first he had dismissed the thought as "not practical." As fond as he was of Ned, he needed an older boy. As the weeks went on, he saw how Martha flourished as a kind of mother to the boy, and he began to realize that it would break her heart if Ned were sent away. And at last he came to know himself: it would break his own heart as well. But, being a cautious man, he had not communicated these thoughts to Martha or Ned, "in case we might not keep him after all." He had put off making a final decision from day to day, until here at last, he must make a choice. Mr. Owen was waiting for an answer.

"I don't know that it would be convenient," said Sam.

"Oh? Would you like to wait another week?"

"The fact is, Mr. Owen," said Sam slowly, "You can't have Ned." He felt three pairs of eyes on him and it seemed that the world was holding its breath.

"Can't have him?" said Mr. Owen.

"No," said Sam. "You can't have him. He's our boy now." His eyes met Ned's and the expression in them made Sam want to weep. He had never seen a look so full of joy and relief. He dared not look at Martha, lest he break down completely.

Mr. Owen understood then that that he was witnessing the birth of a family, and his heart was too glad to leave room for any other emotion.

"Well," he said, fighting back tears himself, "that's fine. We'll find another place for Ralph easily enough." He shook hands with Mr. Johnson and Ned, nodded to Mrs. Johnson, and got back into his buggy. He clucked to the horse and tightened the reigns, tipping his hat to the family as he left the farmyard.

"'God setteth the solitary in families'," he quoted to himself, "'Blessed be God.'"

Epilogue

Ned stayed with the Johnsons, and was known as "the Johnson boy." As they had no children, he inherited the farm when he was twenty-five. He married a local girl and settled down to raise cattle and crops. In his later years, surrounded by his five children and 27 grandchildren, he would say that his only regret was that he had not been able to further his education. Like most boys in that time and place, he left school when he was fourteen. However, he was a great reader all his days and two of his sons went to university.

Ralph Shaw was removed from the Webster farm and given a different placement, where he was treated more kindly. Jack and Dick both did well, although neither was adopted by the farmers they worked for.

Katie and Emmy grew up in the Girls Village and both became housemaids in England. Katie was a trusted servant for years, and Emmy married a butcher when she was twenty.

Mr. Langley married Miss Coulson the next year and emigrated to Canada. He pastored a rural church and was the best friend that the emigrant children in his area ever had.

Historical notes

All the things that happen to Ned in this book actually happened to various children in that time and those places, although Ned is fictional and I do not think all these things ever happened to the same child!

Chapter 2

Because this is a book for children, I have left out a lot of unsavoury detail regarding life in London's East End in Victorian times. There was prostitution (even child prostitution), immorality of all kinds, gambling, violence and foul language that I have not felt compelled to describe in any detail. Therefore, be assured that life for a homeless child in London's East End was worse than I have depicted in this story.

Sometimes the illegitimate children of poor women (often factory workers) were given over to the care of "baby farmers." These were women who took care of the babies for a small fee per week. Almost always the babies were mistreated (starved and abused) and very few lived long at all. If the birthmother could no longer afford to pay, the baby was killed (usually smothered). Often the birthmothers knew exactly what would happen to their children, but occasionally they were deceived about what was really going on. Some of them genuinely believed that the lady really wanted to adopt a child.

Sometimes toddlers would be handed over to a baby farmer for a set amount of money. The baby farmer would keep the money and take the child to a strange part of London and leave him there. This is what happened to Ned. They often got the nickname "nobody's children" because they appeared to come from nowhere. (See "Bastardy and Baby Farming in Victorian England" by Dorothy L. Haller)

Chapter 7

The name of the governor of the Boys Home in the early 1880's is given in different documents as Mr. Field, Rev. Fielding, and Mr. Fielder. While it is possible that there were three different men with these names who were all governors of the Home in the space of a very few years, I think it more likely that two of them are mistakes. My apologies to anyone connected with that honoured gentleman if I have chosen the wrong version of his name.

Chapter 16

I have been slightly inaccurate in having Ned go to Hazelbrae in April of 1884: it was actually a few months later that Hazelbrae opened its doors for the first time to Barnardo children. However, it was such a prominent part of the Barnardo work in Canada for so many years that I just could not leave it out of the story. Later in the 1880's it was the receiving Home just for the girls; the boys went to a Home in Toronto.

Chapter 20

Abuse of varying degrees was, sadly, common among "Home children." Even where there was no actual mistreatment, these immigrant children were often extremely lonely and received no affection from their employers. Some were treated as second-class citizens, not being able to eat with the family and sleeping in poor quarters. Many girls were compromised either by their employers or by hired hands working at the farms. Some child immigrant agencies had no visitation system at all, and the children were at the mercy of their employers. Among the agencies that did follow up on their placements (like Barnardo's), some visitors were more thorough than others. Some visitors merely talked to the farmer and took his word for things, while others talked to the children separately and took seriously what the children said.

Undoubtedly, some children's lives changed for the worse when they went to Canada, and some remained in miserable circumstances their whole lives. Others went from a difficult situation in England to a difficult situation in Canada; most of them do seem to have done well once they reached maturity and were able to be out on their own. And then there were some, like Ned, who started life in terrible conditions, rose into a more comfortable position at a Home like Barnardo's, and then found a real home and family in Canada. It was probably not usual, but it did happen.

"Barnardo's" is still a charity organization in the United Kingdom, though the last resident homes for children were closed in the 1970's. Barnardo's works with underprivileged children and are active in legislation regarding children. They are no longer an evangelical Christian institution, and the primary aim of Dr. Barnardo—to bring boys and girls to salvation in Jesus Christ—would undoubtedly be viewed with distaste by the organization.

Made in the USA
Charleston, SC
27 September 2011